MATTHEW MUDDLES THROUGH

Book 1 in the Matthew in the Middle Series

to: Mom

Glenda Faye Mathes

Glenda Faye Mathes

Matthew Muddles Through (Matthew in the Middle #1)

Copyright © 2014

Glenda Faye Mathes

http://ascribelog.wordpress.com/

Cover design by Ken Raney, Clash Creative, Inc.

http://kenraneyartandillustration.blogspot.com/

Scripture quotations are from The Holy Bible, New International Version, NIV®, Copyright © 1973, 1978, 1984 by International Bible Society. Used by permission. All rights reserved worldwide.

This novel is a work of fiction. Names, characters, businesses, places, events and incidents are either the products of the author's imagination or used in a fictitious manner. Any resemblance to actual persons, living or dead, or actual events is purely coincidental. Author Sigmund Brouwer graciously granted permission for his character as depicted.

References to the 1996 Cadet International Camporee reflect facts regarding its location, requirements, and events, but all scenes are imaginary. For more information about the Calvinist Cadet Corps, see its website: http://www.calvinistcadets.org/

ISBN: 1502836130

ISBN-13: 9781502836137

DEDICATION

For Gabe,
the first person to hear and love
Matthew's story

Dear Reader,

As a middle child, Matthew Vos struggles with an annoying younger brother and an obnoxious older brother. A big-as-a-bear neighborhood dog targets him like a heat-seeking missile. His Cadet Club crams into the church's too-small basement, and his catechism class meets in his living room. He longs to attend the 1996 Cadet International Camporee, but will he even get the chance? How can he rescue his mom's book from the principal's "Black Hole"? And why does Mom feel so sick all the time?

Because Matthew's a Preacher's Kid, whose family is part of a Dutch Reformed church, and because almost all the action takes place in 1996, you'll notice some differences between his life and yours. But many of his problems, thoughts, and feelings will seem familiar.

Join Matthew as he muddles through.

Happy reading!

– Mrs. Mathes

Dear Parent:

Matthew Muddles Through is the first book in a three-volume series that realistically portrays a specific religious and ethnic community (Dutch Reformed) as it existed in 1996 and continues to flourish within small geographical pockets in the United States and Canada. Although worship services and family devotions have changed in many places, the practices as depicted in this story are still observed by many churches and families.

The setting and characters are fictional, but truthful to real-life experience. These books transport the reader into the life of an ordinary, but imaginative boy—a Preacher's Kid—surrounded by complex people and personal problems that help him grow in many ways.

The novels are aimed at middle grade boys, but anyone can enjoy them. Within the context of an engaging story, readers learn about handling problems, valuing others, overcoming fears, and trusting God.

– Glenda Faye Mathes

NOISE IN THE NIGHT

I sat up with my heart pounding. My little brother, Luke, lay on his own side of the bed, curled like a baby. He couldn't have woken me. The streetlamp shone through the window, making a tilted rectangle of light on the floor of our room like it did every night.

Nothing's wrong, I told myself. *Go back to sleep.*

A gagging noise—like someone choking—echoed up the stairs and into the hall.

Someone is choking to death!

I threw back the blankets and dashed downstairs. Seeing the bathroom light on, I ran to the open door. Mom sat on the floor, her head in her hands and hair hanging over her face.

"Mom." I took one step into the room. "You okay?"

She lowered her hands and looked up. Strands of black hair over her white face looked like a zebra. She gathered her hair behind her neck, and her lips quivered into a small smile. But her face was still as white as the snow on the ground surrounding our house.

"I'm all right, Matthew." Her voice quavered. "Sorry to wake you."

"What's wrong?" I stepped back. "You got the flu?"

"I'm not sure." She wiped her mouth with a Kleenex. "Maybe just something I ate."

"That pizza was kind of spicy." Although the four pieces I'd eaten hadn't bothered me.

Mom stood to wash her face, then rinsed the cloth and held it against her forehead. She smiled in the mirror at me. "I feel better now. You should go back to bed. It's too early to get up."

I yawned. "What time is it?"

She was less pale. "I think only about 4:30."

I walked into the kitchen and checked the stove clock. "It's 4:43."

"I thought so." Mom came out of the bathroom, tying the belt on her blue robe. "Too early for you to be up. Go back to bed."

"Okay. If you're sure you're all right."

Mom sat in her recliner in the den. "I'll stay down here for a while." She closed her eyes. "Maybe I can get a little more sleep."

Up in my room, Luke sprawled across the whole bed. I shoved him off my side. Every night he kicked my legs or kneed my back or slapped my face—like I was his personal punching bag.

I pulled my fair share of the blankets over me. The window light glinted in the glass of the family photo on my desk. Grandpa Weaver took that picture at the beach last year when we visited him and Grandma in Florida. I remembered the greenish-blue waves surging on the tan sand and the white gulls with black-tipped wings shrieking in the blue sky.

In the picture, Mom held Luke in front of her by his shoulders. He scowled beneath the brim of a yellow hat and clutched a toy red shovel and green bucket. John slouched beside Dad, looking cool with his arms crossed over an unbuttoned shirt. Then there was me—with a goofy grin and my hair sticking up—stuck in the middle.

Being in the middle means I'm old enough for work, but too young for fun. I have to clean house while Luke watches TV on Saturday mornings. And I have to stay home when John goes to a movie with his friends.

Luke groaned and flung out his arm. I put up my fists to block him from hitting my face. He leaned his head on my pillow, and I pushed it away. That kid drools as bad as Brutus, our neighbor's big-as-a-bear dog.

The squeaky third step creaked. Soft footsteps shuffled past our room, and a door clicked shut. Mom must be feeling better. Maybe it had been the pizza.

Outside, in the cone of light beneath the streetlamp, tiny snowflakes fluttered down like glittering diamonds.

For the first few weeks of winter, I'd been excited every time it snowed. But now Christmas was past, and only a few days were left in 1995. Soon it would be 1996, the year of the Cadet International Camporee.

I hope I'm old enough to make the cut-off date.

For three years—ever since John had gone—I'd been longing to go to Camporee. Cadets and counselors from all over the United States and Canada build their own shelters and camp for a week. It comes around only once every three years. I'd heard this one would be in the mountains. I'd never even seen mountains.

Under the light, fluffy snowflakes floated down like feathers from a burst pillow.

I finally dropped into sleep and dreamed I was climbing a mountain through a blinding snowstorm. I climbed and climbed, but I could never get to the top.

BIG BROTHER

When I stumbled down the steps the next morning, my older brother John's whine rose from the kitchen. "But, Mom. All my friends are going."

"Maybe." Mom wiped the counter with a dishcloth. "But you absolutely may not skip church for a New Year's Eve party." She glanced up at me. "Good morning, Matt."

"Morning, Mom. Morning, John."

John grunted and spooned in a mouthful of cereal.

A cartoon video played on the den TV. Luke sat cross-legged in front of it with his mouth hanging open. On my way to the kitchen, I touched his shoulder. "Morning, Luke." He didn't even grunt. My brothers are so friendly.

"New Year's Eve comes only once a year." John gestured with his spoon. "It isn't going to kill me to miss one measly church service—especially in the evening."

Mom scrubbed at a spot. "If I were you, I wouldn't let your father hear you say that."

"Let me hear you say what?" Dad stood in the hall. I hadn't noticed his study door opening and was pretty sure Mom and John hadn't heard it either.

"Nothing." John filled his mouth with cereal.

I opened the cereal cabinet. "Any Fruit Loops?"

"You know I never buy those sugary cereals." Mom tossed her cloth into the sink. Suds splashed the faucet.

Dad faced my brother and crossed his arms. "Let's hear it, John. What did you say?"

John swallowed. "I just asked to go to the New Year's Eve party at the Clarks' house."

Dad looked at Mom. She frowned. "There was a little more to it than that."

I poured milk in my bowl. "He said it wasn't going to kill him to miss one measly evening church service."

John whipped his head. "Thanks a lot, tattletale!"

"Don't shout at him." Dad lifted one hand. "Or call him names. I'd have found out what you said whether or not he told me."

"It wouldn't hurt if I missed a church service for once," John said. "Lots of people miss evening services."

Dad shrugged. "If lots of people jumped off a cliff, would you do it, too?"

"Course not." John sighed. "But it's New Year's Eve. There'll probably be a ton of empty pews Sunday night."

"All the more reason for you to be there."

John pushed back his chair. "It's not like I'm going to lose my faith or anything by missing one service. You always say that going to church doesn't save anybody."

"It doesn't." Dad's lips formed a firm line. "But you may recall me saying that people who are saved *want* to go to church."

I stopped shoveling in Wheaties. I didn't always want to go to church.

John's face flamed radish red. He stared at the table. "But all my friends are going—"

"Are the Howard twins going?" My eyebrows rose in surprise. "Last week on the bus, Rachel said they were going to play their violins at our New Year's Eve service."

John twisted toward me. "You stay out of this."

"That's enough, John." Dad bent forward to put his hands on the table. "Rachel and Rebekah's string quartet *is* scheduled to play Sunday evening. Are they planning to attend this party after church?"

"I don't know." John glanced at Dad and then looked down again. "Guess not."

"I didn't think their parents would let them go." Dad straightened. "So apparently not quite all your friends are going."

"No, not quite all."

"John, even if this party didn't conflict with a worship service, we wouldn't let you go." Dad crossed his arms. "For one thing, freshmen are too young for such parties."

Mom drained the sink. "For another thing, you're not allowed to stay out after midnight."

Dad nodded. "And these parties are almost always an excuse for excess."

"Drinking, you mean?" John frowned. "There wouldn't be any alcohol."

"Maybe not." Dad rubbed his chin. "But we don't know the Clarks and we don't know how well this party will be chaperoned."

"Tony is on the JV basketball team with me." John sat up straighter. "He's a good student. He and I were the only players on the honor roll last semester."

"Good for both of you," Dad said. "But I still wonder about chaperones. The Clarks haven't called and told us anything about it. How many parents will be there?"

John didn't answer.

"Do you know, John?"

"I'm not sure."

Dad's eyebrows lifted. "You sure you're not sure?"

John squirmed. "Tony said his parents would be at another party."

"Oh, my." Mom put one hand on her cheek. "Do you mean there won't be any parents supervising this party?"

John stared at his empty bowl. "Maybe not."

"That's more than enough reason not to allow you to go." Dad waved his hands like a referee's "no score" at a basketball game. "No room for further discussion." He turned toward Mom. "Lisa, what about having a family party? We can let the kids stay up until midnight since there's no church or school the next day."

Mom put the milk in the refrigerator. "I'm all for that. I can pick up snacks next time I get groceries."

I smacked the table. "We can play games."

John slumped in his chair. "Whoopee."

Dad tilted his head. "Maybe we could see if Uncle Chad and Chris have plans."

"Great idea, Tim," Mom said. "They probably have nothing else to do."

Dad nodded. "People hesitate to invite someone to a party after they've lost a loved one."

"And Pam always arranged their social activities."

"I'll call Chad this evening after he gets off work."

"I hope they can come." Mom picked up the box of Wheaties. "If you guys are finished, stack your dishes in the dishwasher and get dressed."

John jumped up, jammed his bowl and glass on the dishwasher rack, and ran upstairs.

Mom said to Dad, "Somebody's not too happy."

"He'll get over it." Dad clapped his hands together. "I'm going to try to finish my New Year's sermon now that the New Year's party crisis is past."

He rubbed my messy hair, then walked down the hall into his study and closed the door.

Mom looked at me. "Matt, take Luke upstairs and make sure he gets dressed, will you?"

"Do I have to?"

"Now don't *you* start with me, Matthew Henry."

"Oh, all right." I rinsed my bowl at the kitchen sink, staring out the window at the new snow sparkling in the sunshine like a million miniature mirrors.

I was named after Grandpa Weaver and Great-uncle Henry, so my whole name is Matthew Henry Vos. But my mom only uses my middle name when I'm skating on thin ice. And my full name only when I'm in trouble as big as breaking through ice into deep, glacier-cold water.

John was named after Grandpa Vos and Great-uncle Calvin. In Dad's study, he has books by Matthew Henry and John Calvin about the Bible. Some of the kids in our church think it's funny to call us "Matthew Henry" and "John Calvin," especially since our dad's a preacher.

Luke was named after our dad's brothers. Luke Chadwick must not be a famous theologian because no one teases Luke about his name.

"Matthew, stop dreaming. You're wasting water." Mom turned off the faucet. "You're supposed to be taking Luke upstairs to get dressed, remember?"

"Oh, yeah." I scrunched up my face.

My bowl was perfectly clean after that long rinse, but I put it in the dishwasher anyway. I went into the den. Luke still sat like a rock, staring at the screen. If only he'd be that motionless when he was sleeping.

"Luke, let's go upstairs and get dressed."

He didn't move.

"C'mon, Luke." I shook his shoulder. "Mom wants us to get dressed."

Luke stared at me blankly and then back at the TV.

Mom came into the den, picked up the remote, and switched off the TV.

"Hey." Luke jumped up. "What'd you do that for?"

"Time to get dressed, Luke. Go with Matthew. Now."

"Okay, okay." Luke ran up the steps ahead of me.

When I got to the top and turned the corner, John was leaning against the wall. He grabbed my arm and hissed in my face. "Next time I'm having a conversation with Mom and Dad, I'd appreciate it if you kept your little mouth shut."

"All right." I pushed his hand off. "You don't need to get violent."

"If it happens again—" John thumped a fist in his other hand— "I'll show you violent." He stomped down the hall and into his room, slamming the door.

"Matt!" Mom yelled. "Don't slam your door."

"It wasn't me!" I yelled back.

3

MY BIG BOOK PROBLEM

I woke up when Luke bounced out of bed at 6:00. Somehow or other, that kid always knew when it was Saturday and he could watch cartoons. It was my rare chance to have the whole bed to myself and sleep late.

I stretched out my arms and legs.

Wonderful. Saturday and still Christmas vacation.

But soon my brief break would be over and I'd have to go back to fifth grade at John Quincy Adams Middle School. And my Big Book Problem.

It all happened because Mrs. Carter's a terrible teacher. Well, maybe that's not exactly true. But having everyone take turns reading out of the social studies textbook is Boring with a capital B.

So I was reading *The Lion, The Witch and the Wardrobe*, which I had tucked inside my textbook. Twice Mrs. Carter called on me and had to tell me which paragraph to read. But the third time she said my name—which wasn't fair because she never, *ever* calls on anyone three times in one period—she came over to my desk and saw the book. She marched it and me straight to the principal's office.

It was the first time I'd been in Mr. Harding's office, but I wasn't too worried. John had been there plenty of times. Teachers liked him because he was a good student, but he also knew how to push their buttons.

He'd told me that every time he got sent to the principal's office at John Quincy Adams, Mr. Harding tried not to smile while giving him a little lecture. Then he'd put his hand on John's shoulder and walk with him past a smiling secretary. As he shut the office door behind him, John would hear Mr. Harding say to the secretary, "Well, boys will be boys."

When Mrs. Carter led me through the principal's door, she held my book with just her thumb and finger, as if it had germs. "I caught Matthew Vos reading this occult garbage."

"I see." He took the book by the corner and tossed it—without even looking at it—into the big bottom drawer of his desk. John had told me about that drawer. He called it "the Black Hole." Nothing that went into it ever came out again.

Mrs. Carter left, and Mr. Harding gave me a lecture—a real lecture—about applying myself and paying attention. When it was over, he didn't put his hand on my shoulder; he didn't walk me past the secretary; he didn't even get up. He started signing papers on his desk.

I didn't know what to do.

He looked up and said, "That's all. You may go."

I walked back past the secretary, who was typing with tiny headphones in her ears and never even looked at me. Definitely not the John Calvin treatment.

When I told John about it, he just laughed and went outside to shoot baskets. Oh, yeah, I forgot to mention that he's good at sports, too.

But I had a big problem. I had borrowed that book from my dad's study. Every wall is covered with shelves holding all kinds of books, not just religious ones. He usually lets John and me borrow books, as long as we ask. It was just that I hadn't exactly asked this time.

And it was even worse than that. I'd noticed a name written inside the book's front cover: Lisa Weaver. That meant it belonged to my mom before she got married, so it was really old. If my parents found out, I'd be in big trouble. Even bigger than "Matthew Henry Vos" trouble.

Maybe Mom and Dad wouldn't notice for a while. Maybe not until after I graduated from high school and went off to college.

AN EMERGENCY

While I worried about Mom's book, stuck in the Black Hole, John thundered up the steps and into his room.

Mom called, "Matthew, come down here, will you?"

When I walked into the kitchen, the stove clock said 6:30. "Mom, why'd you make me get up so early?"

"Dad's at the hospital, so I need to drive John to basketball practice." Mom rinsed a glass at the sink. "You'll have to watch your little brother for me."

Luke sat at the table in his bright red footie pajamas, eating Cheerios and swinging his legs. The white plastic soles on his feet flashed like a strobe light.

Mom looked different because she was wearing her glasses. She's nearsighted, but almost always wears contacts. "Don't use the stove." She shut the dishwasher. "And don't answer the phone; let the answering machine get it. I should be back in a half hour."

"Couldn't you just prop Luke in front of the TV and let me sleep?"

Mom motioned me into the den.

She whispered, "We're talking about Luke here. Remember the jelly on the curtains?"

"I remember," I whispered back. "It was on more than curtains—window, woodwork, and sofa."

"Don't forget the carpet."

"Right. Probably not a good idea to leave him alone."

"Just keep an eye on him."

"Don't worry. I'll keep him away from the jelly."

"And away from anything else remotely messy or potentially dangerous."

"Got it. No jelly, no knives, no matches."

"Sh-sh. Don't give him any ideas."

I followed her back into the kitchen and had reached the bottom of the stairs, when John barreled down and knocked me over.

"For crying out loud," I hollered from the floor. "Watch where you're going."

"Sorry, bro." He stepped over me. "I was looking in my bag and didn't see you."

I got to my feet. "Be more careful next time."

"I'm running late." John spun around. "Mom, I can't find my jersey. Did you wash it?"

"I think so." Mom took a dirty pan off the burner. "It might still be in the dryer."

John pounded down the basement steps.

Mom started scrubbing the greasy pan, but suddenly leaned on the counter with her head bowed.

I walked around the table. "You okay?"

"My stomach's a little upset." Her face was pale, and she ran water into a glass. "Put your dirty dishes in the dishwasher." She sipped her water. "Luke's, too."

"Okay." I looked in the cabinet for a clean glass.

John ran into the kitchen, stuffing his jersey into his duffle. "Let's go."

"Just a minute." Mom sipped more water.

"Come on, Mom, we've got to go now or I'll be late."

"You can wait a minute." I slammed the cabinet door.

"I don't have a minute. I can't be late for practice or I'll lose my place on the team."

"And that's more important than Mom?"

John rolled his eyes. "Give me a break."

"Cut it out, you two." Mom picked up her purse. "I'm ready to go now, John."

"Can I drive?" John had his learner's permit, but he hadn't taken Driver's Ed yet.

"*May* I drive," Mom corrected.

"Well, may I then?"

Mom took the keys from the hook by the back door and eyed him. "I've always felt that driving instruction was a father thing."

"Oh, come on, Mom." John whined like a little kid. "I've driven with Dad lots of times."

Mom handed him the keys, and he sprinted out the door. She looked around as if it might be the last time she saw her home. I knew how she felt—I'd ridden in the car with John driving.

"Okay." She took a deep breath and put her hand on my shoulder, almost as though she hoped I'd always remember her. "Don't forget about the dishes."

"I won't."

Just as she turned the doorknob, the car horn beeped. "Oh, no, John. The neighbors. It's not even 7:00." She hurried out.

After the door closed behind her, I narrowed my eyes at Luke. "Eat your Cheerios."

"You're not my boss." Luke's mouthful of mushy cereal and milk made it sound like, "Yournamabosh."

"I am for now." I scooped dry Cheerios from the box and popped them into my mouth.

"Hey." Luke scowled. "Don't do that."

"Says who?"

"I'll tell Mom."

"Go ahead." He'd probably forget before Mom got back. But I decided to make sure. I patted a chair. "If you sit here, you can see the TV in the den."

Luke scooted over and I shoved his bowl and glass in front of him. Then I went into the den, picked up the remote, and flipped through channels until I found an old Warner Brothers cartoon. Luke watched like a zombie, eating only during commercials.

I snuck into Dad's study and checked the shelf in the corner. An empty space gaped between *That Hideous Strength*, the last of the Space Trilogy, and *Prince Caspian*, the second in The Chronicles of Narnia series. I pulled the Narnia book off the shelf and looked at the cover. A man and boy were fighting with swords and shields. It looked exciting, but I reluctantly put it back in place. I didn't want to read the series out of order, and I felt guilty about losing Mom's book. I spread out the books, so the empty space wasn't as big.

Dad's computer was on. I played Solitaire until I won a game. I loved watching the cards flip out—as if someone had pinched the stacks between their fingers—and leave tracks of outlines like a slow cartoon.

Cartoon. I'd better check on Luke.

I closed the "Games" window and left the study.

Luke still stared at the TV, but the Cheerios in his bowl were gone.

I snapped my fingers in his face. "Finish your milk."

He put his bowl to his lips and slurped the sludge.

"Drink your juice."

He lifted his glass and gulped his warm orange juice.

"Jump two feet."

He looked at me.

"Just kidding."

After I picked up his dishes and put them in the dishwasher, I watched cartoons with him.

There was one about two goofy gophers who lived in a tree and gathered nuts like squirrels. Their tree was cut down and taken into a noisy lumber mill. A loud buzz saw sliced the tree—and almost them. At the end, their "tree" was a tall stack of furniture. It was pretty funny.

The news came on, so Luke got down from his chair.

I turned off the TV. "Maybe you should get dressed."

"Maybe you should." Luke pointed at me. "You're still in PJs, too."

"Okay, we'll both get dressed." That way I could make sure he left my stuff alone.

In our room, I tossed Luke a sweatshirt and jeans. Then I handed him a pair of clean socks. I finally found my favorite pair of jeans and dug through my drawer for a warm sweatshirt.

While I pulled the shirt over my head, a loud pop startled me. Luke screamed.

DEATH DEFIED

I stuck my head out of my shirt. The lights were out. Smoke clouded the air. It smelled weird—sort of like burning lemons.

Luke lay on the floor, kicking and shrieking. I fell to my knees beside him and felt all over his arms and legs for broken bones.

"Luke, Luke, you all right?"

"I didn't mean to, I didn't mean to!"

He didn't seem hurt, so I pulled him from our room and down to the kitchen, where the light was still on.

Luke was crying and his nose was running. He had on his jeans and shirt, but no socks. I didn't see any blood. But his hair stuck straight up all over his head.

I got a Kleenex from the bathroom and wiped his snotty nose. "What happened, Luke?"

"I-I'm sorry, I d-didn't mean to do it." He began blubbering harder.

"Do what?"

Luke wailed and put his hands over his face.

"Stay here," I said. "I'm going up to check for fire."

He shrieked, but I was not as worried about him as I was about our house.

I yelled as I ran, "Stop crying and stay put!"

There was still a funny smell in our room, but I didn't see any smoke. No flames. What had made that noise?

Our Superman night-light lay on the floor. A wire clothes hanger rested on its metal prongs. Had Luke messed with wire and the outlet? Was he that dumb?

I picked up the hanger and the night-light and went to the window to look at them. The picture of Superman was almost completely blacked out by a big burn spot.

When I got back in the kitchen, Luke was still crying. He needed a tissue again.

I had no sympathy. I held up the hanger and night-light. "What did you do, Luke?"

He cried harder, and snot poured from his nose. It was gross.

I got the box of tissues from the bathroom and shoved it in his face. "Now, before Mom gets home, wipe your nose and tell me what you did."

"I—I—wanted t-to p-play with S-Superman." Luke dabbed at his snotty nose. "I—I—c-couldn't g-get him off the wall so I t-tried—t-to p-pull him off with the hanger." He hiccuped.

"Don't you know electricity is dangerous?" I wrapped a tissue around his nose. "Blow."

He blew. He looked at me with wide eyes. "I d-didn't know it would d-do that."

"C'mon." I tossed the dirty tissues into the kitchen wastebasket. "Let's get your socks on. Then we'd better comb our hair and brush our teeth."

Luke calmed down while I combed his hair. I used about a gallon of water to make it stay down. I put minty fresh Crest on each of our toothbrushes, and we began brushing our teeth.

The back door slammed, and Mom ran into the bathroom.

"Out," she ordered with a face white as Elmer's glue.

With a mouth full of foam, I asked, "That bad, was it?"

"Out!"

We spit, rinsed, and split.

Mom was in the bathroom with the door shut for a long time. When she came out, she looked better and even smiled a little. "Sorry for yelling."

Luke looked worried. "You okay, Mommy?"

"I'm okay—now."

I asked, "What's wrong?"

"Oh, nothing much," she said, "aside from that brother of yours practically getting both of us killed."

"How did he do that?"

"He nearly pulled out in front of a garbage truck—"

"Wow."

"—and about sideswiped two parked cars."

"I almost wish I could have seen it—almost."

"Be glad you didn't." Mom plopped on a kitchen chair. "From now on, I'm leaving driving instruction to Dad."

I cleared my throat. "You might want to check the electricity upstairs."

Mom looked at me in surprise. "Why would I want to do that?"

"Because Luke made it go off."

She sat up straight. "What happened?"

Luke started crying again. I held up the hanger and night-light. "Luke tried to pry the night-light off the outlet with this wire hanger."

"Oh, my." Mom grabbed Luke. "Are you all right?"

"He's okay," I said, "but the night-light is shot, and the upstairs electricity is out."

"He probably tripped a circuit breaker. I'll go downstairs and flip the switch."

She hugged the bawling baby. "Luke, Luke, you could have hurt yourself."

"Mom." I shook my head. "He could have hurt more than himself. He could have killed us both and burned down the house."

"Now, Matthew." Mom let go of Luke and patted my head. "You're overreacting again."

Easy for her to say. She hadn't been nearly fried.

6
THE DREADED LIST

Mom sent me upstairs while she went to the basement and flipped breakers. For the first time ever, she told me to shout. She found the right one and the lights came back on, so I yelled with full lung power.

When we were both back in the kitchen, she asked, "What are your plans for the day?"

Well, I really didn't have any plans—it was Christmas vacation, after all. So Mom wrote out a list of chores. She's always been a great one for making lists.

First I had to clean the bathroom sink. Globs of toothpaste were stuck in it from our quick rinse. Then I made our bed and took down our dirty laundry. After that, I had to practice piano for a half hour. Helping Mom take the Christmas ornaments off the tree and pack them in Rubbermaid containers might have been fun, if Luke hadn't been making such a racket while he was allowed to play with his new Thomas the Tank Engine train set.

When we finished stripping the tree, I carried the ornament containers up to the attic. Then I had to take the tree to the curb. I put on my winter coat, stocking cap, and bulky snow boots. Mom handed me an old pair of gloves so I wouldn't get sap on my good ones. At every step on the way to the street, the tree dropped dry pine needles. When I tossed it down, the needles showered on the white snow and formed a brown mound. That skimpy tree looked pretty pathetic, lying lopsided with a few strands of silver tinsel icicles fluttering in the breeze.

Even after all that, the sun was still low. It looked like a shimmering white Frisbee disk. Nothing like the golden ball I'd seen in Florida last year, glowing above the sparkling sea and warm sand.

I was born in Florida, but I don't remember living there because we moved to Iowa when I was only a baby. When we visited Grandpa and Grandma last year, John remembered palm trees and swimming in the ocean. He plans to move back when he grows up, so he doesn't have to put up with "miserable Midwestern winters" anymore.

Now new snow from last night covered big piles of old snow lining the driveway. The lumps were beginning to melt, and little rivers of water ran down the concrete. I kicked the biggest mound by the garage. The hole left by my boot toe looked like a cave in a mountain.

I wondered if taking out the tree had been the last thing on Mom's list. I kicked deeper holes that could be caves for my toy soldiers.

Why is Mom feeling so sick? Aunt Pam was sick all the time before she died last year. John told me that cancer runs in families.

I kicked harder.

Dad drove up. He shut the car door and stretched. He smiled, but under his eyes he had half moon shadows.

"Hi, Dad. You been up all night?"

"No, just most of it." Dad jerked off my stocking cap. "You hardly even need this today."

"So what was up at the hospital?"

"An elderly gentleman thought he was dying and wanted to talk to me."

"Was he dying?"

"Well, strictly speaking, we all are."

"Yeah, yeah, I know." Dad often tried to make me think about God, but I didn't want to get into a religious discussion. I wanted to know about the old guy. "But is the man dead?"

"Not yet."

"Why'd he want to talk to you all night?"

"Just part of it," Dad reminded me. "He wanted to discuss assurance."

"He's dying and he wants to talk about theology?"

"He wanted to be sure he was really saved. That when he died he would go to heaven."

"Why would he wonder about that? Doesn't he believe in Jesus?"

"Yes, he believes in Jesus."

"Then he's going to heaven. It's simple, isn't it?"

"The faith of a child." Dad put my stocking cap back on my head, pulling it down over my eyebrows. "Sometimes older people can't stop thinking about their past sins and failures. It's hard for them to believe God can forgive them."

"I don't get it, Dad." I pushed the cap up.

"You don't have to. Just keep believing in Jesus and living for him."

That reminded me of our Cadet theme song. After Dad went into the house, I started singing: "Living for Jesus a life that is true, Striving to please Him in all that

I do, Yielding allegiance, glad hearted and free, This is the pathway of blessing for me."

Nobody was around, so I sang louder: "O Jesus, Lord and Savior, I give myself to You; For You, in Your atonement, Did give Yourself for me. I own no other Master, My heart shall be Your throne. My life I give, henceforth to live, O Christ, for You alone."

I'd been kicking the snow pile and by the time I finished that chorus—which is pretty lively—I realized I was singing *real* loud. I looked around, but none of the neighbors stood outside and I didn't see anybody peering out their windows.

I took off my cap and went inside.

A QUESTION

I threw my arms out, balancing on bobbing logs in a roaring river. The bucking logs bounced around a bend and I spotted the cave-like opening of a lumber mill. A noise—louder than an angry grizzly—roared from the dark hole. Logs disappeared into it like toothpicks sucked into a bear's mouth. Slippery timbers rolled beneath my feet, and I fell flat on my belly. I clung to a log, but the current flung it forward in a rushing wave—straight toward a buzzing blade!

I sat up trembling. My heart pounded. I wasn't lying on a log heading toward spinning teeth—I was in bed. Beside me, Luke snored as loudly as a lumber mill saw.

I hopped up and pawed through my underwear drawer until I found a stretched-out tube sock. I slipped it under Luke's chin and tied it in a double knot at the top of his head. Maybe that would hold his mouth shut and keep him from snoring.

Water ran somewhere downstairs, probably Dad or Mom in the shower. Dad always showered before breakfast, but Mom did too on Sunday morning so the water in the heater had time to warm up again before John and I took showers. Dad would call us soon.

Maybe I could read in peace before he called. It'd be better than lying awake beside the muzzled buzz saw.

I sat at my desk and turned on my lamp. Luke moaned and flung an arm on my side of the bed.

Ha! Missed me.

I examined my stack of library books. *Phantom Outlaw at Wolf Creek* by Sigmund Brouwer had been great, and I wanted to find more of those Accidental Detectives books the next time I went to the library.

I picked up a book about special operations forces. They're military teams with extra training, who are sent on risky or secret missions. If they don't want their whispers overheard, they make a "th" sound instead of an "s" sound so the hissing doesn't give them away.

That book reminded me of *The Visual Dictionary of Special Military Forces*, which I'd gotten for Christmas. I found it and opened it. The first page showed a German World War II submarine. I knew the tube for looking above water was the periscope, but I learned the bump on the top with the hatch is called the conning tower.

"You're up early, Matt." Dad stood in our doorway, knotting his tie.

"Luke's snoring woke me up," I said. "Can't I move in with John?"

"We've been through all this before." Dad sighed. "John has the smaller room and the smaller bed. You just have to live with it. Unless—"

"Unless, what?"

"Never mind. I shouldn't have said anything yet."

"Said anything about what?"

"The Building and Grounds Committee has come up with a new proposal, and the council will vote on it next Monday. That's really all I should say for now, Matt."

Then he said loudly, "Time for breakfast, Luke." He called down the hall, "Rise and shine, John."

Luke sat up and blinked. The sock knot on top of his head looked like floppy bunny ears.

"Mernim, Mam," he mumbled. He knit his eyebrows together and put his hands to his cheeks. He touched the sock around his face, grasped it, and jerked it off. "Morning, Matt."

"Morning, Luke." I stood and shut off my desk lamp. "Breakfast time."

I paused at the door and glanced back. Luke was staring at the tied tube sock in his hands.

In the hall, I pretended I was on a special operations mission. I squatted and peered down the stairs. Dad walked into his study. From the way dishes rattled, Mom must be setting the table. I hugged the wall and tiptoed on the sides of the steps, skipping the squeaky third one.

When I reached the bottom, I peeked into the kitchen. Mom was dressed for church, except for her shoes, which she never put on until she was ready to walk out the door. She looked pretty funny, wearing her best dress and panty hose with fuzzy pink slippers.

A carton of juice, the milk jug, and some cereal boxes already crowded the table. When Mom turned her back, I dashed down the hall. Dad's office chair wheels squeaked. I slipped into the bathroom and quietly closed the door. I'd made it all the way without being seen.

While I washed my hands, I thought about what Dad had said. *How could a new proposal possibly get me out of sharing a room with Luke?*

In the kitchen, Mom and Luke sat at the table. Mom held a sleeve of saltines.

Luke whined, "I'm hungry."

"Hush, Luke. Here, eat this." Mom handed him a cracker. "We'll have breakfast in a minute." She looked pale. She took out another cracker and nibbled on it.

Dad came into the kitchen with his suit jacket in one hand and his Bible in the other. He set his Bible by his place. Then he pulled out his chair and hung his jacket on it. He was about to sit, when Mom said, "Tim."

"What, honey?"

"John's not here."

Dad looked at John's empty place and sighed.

I poured myself a glass of juice. "He was probably reading late again last night."

Mom and Dad looked at me.

"If I shared a room with him, he would have to turn off the light and go to sleep on time."

"Nice try." Dad's lips twisted to one side. "Why don't you run upstairs and wake him?"

When I came into John's room, he was sleeping with his head under his pillow.

I tiptoed to his bed and leaned down, close to where I thought his ear would be.

"John!" I sprinted toward the door and turned my head. "Time to get up!"

John sat up and glared at me.

I stepped back. "Dad sent me up. We're waiting for you."

He lifted his pillow and I ran. The pillow sailed into the hall and landed on the floor behind me. I dashed down the steps.

I slid onto my chair and caught my breath. "He'll be right down."

Mom frowned. "You didn't have to shout."

"Oh." I took a sip of juice. "You heard that?"

Dad added, "All our neighbors probably heard it."

John walked slowly into the kitchen and stood beside his chair. His eyes narrowed and his nostrils flared. With a nose ring, he'd have looked like the bull on one of Luke's cartoons.

Dad tapped the table. "Take your seat, John."

"I'd appreciate it," John spat every word through clenched teeth, "if you wouldn't send Matt to wake me."

"I'm sure you would." Dad's smile was a thin line. "But you have to admit, it was effective."

Mom tilted her head at Dad. "Maybe you should go next time, Tim."

Dad turned. "John, why don't you just make sure there isn't a next time?"

"How can I do that?"

Dad shrugged. "You can come for breakfast the first time I call."

"What if I don't hear you?"

I looked at John. "You could set your alarm."

He jerked toward me. "You could shut your mouth."

"Actually," Mom said, "I think setting your alarm is a good idea."

"So do I." Dad nodded. "You have to learn to get yourself up every day."

"I don't want to set my alarm on the one day I can sleep in."

"Set it later than usual." Dad put his hands together. "Let's pray."

After prayer, Mom poured Cheerios into Luke's bowl.

John asked, "No eggs and bacon?"

Mom shook her head. "Not this morning. Maybe tomorrow."

Dad flung his tie over his shoulder so he wouldn't spill food on it. "Well, kids, this is your last day of vacation from church school. Classes begin again next Sunday."

"Who will be my teacher?" Luke spluttered mushy sludge.

"Don't talk with your mouth full, dear," Mom said. "It will be Mrs. Sawyers, just like before Christmas."

"Don't I get a new teacher?"

"No."

"But you're going to be a new teacher for the babies."

"The babies?" Dad wrinkled his forehead. "You're only in kindergarten, Luke. You were in that class last year. Call it what it is, the preschoolers."

"Okay, the preschoolers. But don't I get a new teacher?"

"No, Mom's the only new teacher. She's just finishing the year for Mrs. Larson."

"Why?"

"Mrs. Larson hasn't been feeling well because she's going to have a baby," Dad spoke slowly. "A tiny baby who won't be big enough to go to Sunday school for at least three years."

Dad didn't say the real reason Mom was filling in for Mrs. Larson, but I knew.

The real reason was Mom didn't like being in the house while my catechism class met there. We came in the back door and walked through the kitchen into the living room. A narrow sidewalk connected the church and our house, which everybody called "the parsonage."

Our church is old and doesn't have many classrooms. Since some new families joined last summer, there wasn't enough space for all the classes in the fall. So fifth grade catechism had to meet in my house.

A few weeks ago I'd heard Mom talking to Dad.

"It's downright unnerving to have a bunch of kids trekking back and forth through the kitchen while I'm preparing lunch," she'd said. "If I take over for Holly Larson, I won't even be in the house during Sunday school and I think I'll be happier."

"Good idea," Dad had replied. "But do you have time for all the preparation?"

"The helper does the crafts, so I only need to prepare the lesson. I can handle that."

Then they'd noticed me playing with my little green soldiers in the front hall and began talking loudly about what to have for dinner.

If my parents talk loud enough to hear, it's probably not important. It's when they talk quietly that it gets interesting. Then I usually pretend to be busy playing or reading.

Now Dad poured milk on his Wheaties. "Who's going to be your helper, dear?"

"I'm not sure," Mom said. "Amy Williams was helping Holly, but she transferred to Iowa State this semester so she won't be around."

"Is the Youth Education Committee aware of that?"

"Frank gave me some names to call. I'll find someone. Eat your cereal, Matthew."

8

A THREAT

After devotions, Dad put on his suit jacket, picked up his Bible, and left for church. He walks over early to pray with the elders and deacons before each service.

"Luke," Mom said, "bring down your Sunday clothes and I'll help you get ready."

I put my bowl in the dishwasher. "You're helping him get ready down here?"

"I'll supervise him while cleaning up breakfast." She poured detergent in the dishwasher's cup. "I want to avoid a repeat performance of the night-light incident."

If I hurried with my shower, I might have some time alone in my room. Before Luke had found his socks, I'd grabbed my church clothes and rushed back down to the bathroom. I showered in hyperdrive. Then I ran upstairs and flopped onto the bed. I put my hands behind my head and sighed. *Just think—this is what it would be like to have a room to myself all the time.*

The door shut. John leaned against it, holding his Sunday clothes in crossed arms.

"Oh, hi, John." I sat up. "How's it going?"

"How do you think it's going, moron?"

"Hey!"

John walked over to the bed and leaned over me. His face was white. He hissed, "I am sick and tired of you butting in where you don't belong."

I scooted like a crab to the other side of the bed. "What do you mean?"

"You know what I mean, little brother. You're always sticking your nose into my business and saying things you've got no right to say."

"Am I?" I inched back a bit.

"You know very well you are, and you had better knock it off."

"Okay."

John went to the door and opened it. Then he turned and looked at me. "I mean it." He jabbed his finger at me. "You stay out of my business."

He shut the door and stomped down the steps.

I put on socks and shoes and hurried downstairs. Mom rinsed a dishcloth in the sink.

"How cold is it?" I asked. "Do I need gloves?"

She looked out the window at the thermometer on the clothesline pole.

"No, it's above freezing. But wear your winter coat. And stay on the sidewalk so your good shoes don't get muddy. Where's your Bible and sermon notebook?"

"Oh, I forgot." I ran upstairs to find them. When I came down, Mom was slipping into her high heels and Luke was zipping his parka. I jerked my coat from its hook and slipped it on.

As I left, Mom knocked on the bathroom door. "Get a move on there, John."

I liked living close enough to church that I could walk over by myself. The snow gleamed like an ice sheet floating in the Arctic Ocean. Fence posts cast ladder-like shadows across the walk. I pretended I was climbing the ladder in a submarine's conning tower. I popped through the round opening to suck in fresh air and look around.

The DeWitts' Suburban turned into the lot. They have three girls and two boys. I'm friends with both boys. The one a year younger than me is Drew, but his real name is Andrew. Adam is my age and my best friend. He told me the Chronicles of Narnia were the most interesting books he'd ever read, which was why I'd been so excited to find them on Dad's shelf.

Only now Mom's book was stuck in Mr. Harding's Black Hole vortex.

The DeWitt kids piled out of the Suburban like a bunch of wriggly puppies jumping from a basket. They all ran over to me.

Adam reached me first. "Did you finish *The Lion, the Witch and the Wardrobe*?"

"Matt, my man." Drew slapped my shoulder. "What you been up to?"

"Hi, Matthew." Abigail smiled. "Are you having a nice vacation from school?"

Anna pushed in front of her and asked, "What toys did you get for Christmas?"

Little Ariel held up a pink quilted rectangle. "I got my own Bible and Bible cover."

"Very nice." It was a relief not to be bombarded with a question.

"It's almost like a purse," Ariel said. "See? It has slots for everything—pencils, paper, bookmarks, tissues—even a zippered pocket for my collection money."

"Cool case." I nodded. "Following along in your own Bible will help you learn to read."

"That's just what Mom and Dad said." Ariel put her hand in mine. She was probably used to a brother hanging on to her when they crossed the parking lot.

Her hand felt tiny, like a little doll hand, only warm and soft. And it was nice and clean, not like Luke's grubby paws.

When we got inside the church, we hung up our coats—Adam helped Ariel with hers—and then we stood together at the back, talking about what we'd done over Christmas break. The DeWitts had visited their grand-parents in Colorado and had even gone snow skiing.

Drew smirked. "You should have seen Adam wipe out on the bunny slope."

I wrinkled my forehead. "What's a bunny slope?"

"Only the easiest ski trail."

Abby nodded. "For beginners like us. It's marked with a green circle. Except Drew got bored and went on to the blue squares."

"I even tried a black diamond." Drew spread his arms apart. "As soon as Adam starts down the hill, his skis begin drifting away from each other—"

While Drew told his story, a stranger came into church. He wore a black leather jacket with a red and white patch on the shoulder. He stood at the top of the steps as if he couldn't decide whether to stay or run back down and out the door.

The greeters, Mr. and Mrs. Harris, had their noses buried in their bulletins. Drew threw up his arms and told how the snow flew when Adam fell. Adam shrugged.

The stranger turned. A gray ponytail hung down his jacket between a yellow A and Y.

The DeWitt girls stared. Ariel's mouth dropped open.

I whispered, "Th-top th-taring." Then I leaned toward Ariel. "And clothe your mouth."

Mrs. Armstrong came up the stairs. She'd save the day. She always talked to visitors.

She said, "Good morning," loudly to the stranger, but walked right past him to the Harrises and asked about their visit to their daughter in Boston.

The man stepped back down one step and then another. Mom and Luke came through the door. Mom smiled at the man. She shook his hand and introduced herself. He said his name was Fred Winters. Mom talked about how nice it had been to have a white Christmas and how warm it was for the last day of the year and how quickly the snow was disappearing. Then she said she sure was glad he had joined us for worship and would he like to sit with us?

Mr. Winters smiled. "I'd like that."

What would Dad think when he saw a strange man sitting with his wife and kids?

Mom looked at me, which was my signal to come right away. She looked around. "My oldest son isn't here yet, but we'll just have a seat. He'll find us."

She took Luke's hand and followed the usher down the aisle. I walked behind them and Mr. Winters came after me. The usher handed him a bulletin and he sat on the end, where John usually sat. If Mr. Winters hadn't been there, I could've had that spot for once. Whenever I got the chance, I liked to lean my elbow on the curved arm of the pew.

Mr. Winter's jacket smelled icky, like cigarette smoke. I wiggled closer to Mom.

I found the morning's Scripture text in my Bible. Mr. Winters pointed to the pastor's name on the bulletin and asked aloud, "That your dad?"

"Yes," I whispered.

He looked up front. "Where is he?"

"He meets with the elders and deacons for prayer before the worship service," I whispered even more softly. "He'll be out soon."

John came down the aisle, stopped at our pew, and looked at the man beside me. Mr. Winters looked at him, but didn't move.

I squeezed against Mom to make room for John between Mr. Winters and me.

John stretched his legs over Mr. Winters' knees and stepped on my foot before settling down between us.

He turned and whispered to me, "Who is this guy?"

"Hith name ith Mr. Winterth," I whispered into his ear as quietly as I could.

"Why ith he thitting with uth?" John whispered back.

Mom tapped my knee and scowled.

The organist began playing the prelude. It was "Jesus Shall Reign Where'er the Sun."

The morning light shone through the stained glass windows in bright patches of color. The hair of the people gleamed purple, red, and gold like glowing halos. But Mr. Winters's jacket smelled anything but heavenly.

NEW YEAR'S EVE

That afternoon I read a library book about soldiers in World War I who fought in muddy trenches on the front lines. When I finished the book, I realized I was hungry.

In the kitchen, the clock read 5:00. No wonder I was starving. Mom buttered bread beside the big griddle. I walked to her side. "What's for supper?"

"Grilled cheese sandwiches." She peeled silver paper from a rectangle of Velveeta and cut it with a wire slicer.

"Is that all we're having?"

"And chips." She slipped a cheese slab between two bread slices with the buttered sides out. "Go ahead and get them off the fridge."

I climbed on a chair. "There's a bunch of snacks up here. Can we have Doritos?"

Mom put the buttery sandwich on the hot griddle. "*May* we have Doritos." She got another sandwich ready while the first sizzled. "Those are for our party tonight."

"Doritos, cheese puffs, and potato chips." I hopped down with the chip bag. "I can't believe you bought so much junk food."

Mom grinned. "I had a weak moment in the snack aisle. And in the soda aisle."

"You did?" I opened the refrigerator. "Oh, wow. Root beer and 7-Up."

"There's also a pan of fudge I made last night." She squeezed one eye shut. "We'll stay up all night eating fudge and drinking root beer, my black-hearted friends."

I laughed. "That's what those bad pie-rats say in Luke's Tinker and Tanker book."

"Correct as usual, King Friday."

"Mr. Rogers. The Land of Make-Believe."

Dad came out of his study and folded some papers into his Bible. "Well, I'm ready for this evening's service." He rubbed my hair. "What about you, Matt? Ready to party?"

"Mom said we could stay up all night, eating fudge and drinking root beer."

Dad lifted his eyebrows at Mom.

"It was a joke." She smiled. "And he knows it." She slipped a spatula under a gooey sandwich and flipped it.

I sniffed. "Those smell delicious, Mom."

"Thanks, Matt. But I only made one per person because we'll eat treats after church."

"Can't wait." I opened the chip bag. "Uncle Chad and Chris gonna be here?"

"No." Mom's smile melted away.

"Did you call them, Dad?"

"Yep."

"Don't they want to come?"

"Uncle Chad said they'd like to." Dad rubbed his chin. "But Chris isn't feeling up to it."

"What's wrong? Has he got the flu?"

"No." Dad sighed. "He's been a little depressed since his mom died. Chad said the holidays have been hard. He thought it best if they stayed home."

"If he feels sad, they should come. I bet we'd cheer him up."

"That's what I told him." Dad nodded. "But Chris didn't want to try it."

"His loss." I shrugged. "He'll miss Mom's fudge."

Mom's face was sad. "That might remind him of the mom he misses."

"Maybe so."

Through the whole evening service, I couldn't help thinking about fudge, root beer, and Doritos. Even during the offering, when Rachel and Rebekah Howard played "Another Year Is Dawning" on their violins, my mind sang, *"Lots of snacks to eat and ro-ot beer."*

I left right after church without stopping to talk to Adam, but John still beat me home. When I came in, he was already drinking root beer and eating fudge.

He turned on the TV and flipped through channels until he found one broadcasting from Times Square.

"That's boring." I opened my own can of root beer. "Let's play Clue."

"It doesn't work to play Clue with only two."

"Maybe Mom and Dad will play when they get home." I cut a piece of fudge, just a tiny bit smaller than the empty square John had left.

He turned up the TV volume. "Luke can't read well enough to play."

"Mom always let him be on a team with her."

"I don't know." John swigged soda and stared at the screen. "Last time she said 'never again' because he kept talking about her cards."

"That's why I like him on Mom's team. I don't even have to figure out what she has."

"Speaking of teams." John glared at me. "Mine is at the Clarks right now, having great fun without me, thanks to you."

"That's not my fault. You couldn't go to the party because there weren't going to be any parents—not because of anything I said."

"You didn't help matters any, little brother."

The back door opened. Mom and Dad stood in the doorway, each holding Luke by the hand.

He yelled, "Swing me in."

Mom and Dad counted together. "One, two, three-ee." They lifted Luke and swung him inside.

John shook his head. "No wonder it took you so long to get home."

Mom slipped off her coat and hung it up. "I see you helped yourselves to the root beer." She opened the refrigerator and took out the candy pan. She widened her eyes. "And the fudge."

I pointed at John. "He had the biggest piece."

John sputtered. "Tattletale."

"You two shape up." Mom wagged her finger at us. "John, you don't have to lose your temper so easily with Matt. And Matt, you don't have to always try to get John into trouble."

Do I do that? I walked down the hall to get the Clue game out of the closet.

Dad hung up Luke's coat. "This is supposed to be a fun family time. Make an effort to get along, okay, guys?"

I brought the game up the hall. "Okay."

Dad looked at John, who gulped root beer. He lowered the can. "Okay."

"I think," Mom said, "that each of you should make a New Year's resolution."

Luke asked, "What's a resolution?"

"It's a decision to try to do something better or to begin a good habit," Mom explained. "Like losing weight or reading the Bible every day. People often make resolutions at the beginning of a new year."

John lifted one hand. "I hereby resolve not to lose my temper with Matt." He held the can in front of his mouth and added so quietly only I heard, "as long as he stays out of my hair."

I put the Clue box on the table. "I'll try to get along better with John."

Mom opened a package of paper plates. "I hope you both make the effort."

I lifted the lid off the box. "Clue, anyone?"

Mom frowned. "I don't know."

"What if Luke plays with me?" Dad put his arm around Mom. "I'll keep my cards close."

Mom squeezed his hand. "If you want to do that, I'm up for a game."

Dad turned toward the den. "You in, John?"

"Sure." John shrugged. "But I want to watch TV at 11:00, when the ball drops."

Luke climbed on a chair. "Why does the ball drop, Daddy?"

Dad opened the board. "To mark the new year."

I took out the revolver and aimed it at the clock. "Why at 11:00 instead of midnight?"

"Times Square is in New York City." Dad took the tiny revolver from me and put it in the conservatory on the game board. "So they're an hour ahead of us."

We used magazines to hide our papers and cards from each other. Luke was so busy drinking root beer and eating fudge that he didn't pay attention to Dad's cards.

After several suggestions, I'd figured out the weapon and was pretty sure of the person. But then Mom said, "I'd like to make an accusation."

"Oh," John groaned. "I was going to on my next turn."

"I say it was Mr. Green with the candlestick in the ballroom." Mom pulled the cards from the envelope in the middle of the board. She smiled and laid them face up. "I was right."

John threw down his cards. "I knew it."

I flipped the candlestick in my fingers. "I knew this was the weapon."

Luke said, "I want more fudge."

"You've had plenty." Mom handed him a napkin. "Wipe your mouth. Would you like some grapes?"

"No, I want cheese puffs."

"How do you ask?"

"May I please have cheese puffs?"

"Better." Mom handed me her cards. "You guys put away the game. I'll get snacks."

Dad patted her shoulder. "I'll take care of that."

He poured small helpings of cheese puffs onto our paper plates. "You want any, Lisa?"

"No, thank you." She wrinkled her nose. "I think they taste like cheese-flavored wax."

"How about some Doritos?"

"I'll pass, thanks."

She'd eaten hardly any supper, and I wondered why. "Aren't you hungry? You haven't even had any fudge."

"My stomach's a little queasy. I'll just have a little 7-Up." She looked pale again.

"Why don't we watch a movie?" Dad lifted a video. "I checked out *The Princess Bride* at the library yesterday."

"I love that movie." John poured Doritos on his plate. "No more rhymes, and I mean it."

I finished the joke. "Anybody want a peanut?"

Luke plopped on the sofa, cheese puffs sliding off his plate. "I want a peanut."

"We don't have any." Mom grabbed Luke's tilted plate. "Careful. Those cheese puffs will stain the sofa."

I rolled my eyes. "It's already full of jelly stains."

"I know." She sat on the sofa with Luke. "But we don't have to make it worse."

John sat in Mom's recliner and Dad sat in his. The only place left for me was on the sofa. I heaved a deep sigh. "Do I have to sit beside Luke?"

Dad picked up the remote. "Either sit beside him or get my desk chair from the study."

It was hard to roll that clumsy thing around Dad's desk, but I pretended it was a Gatling gun. I pushed it into position beside the end table, so I'd have a place to set my root beer and plate.

The last person to watch the movie had stopped it in the middle. While it was rewinding, Dad asked, "What do you guys plan to do with your last few days of vacation?"

John said, "Sleep in."

Luke said, "Play."

I said, "Sleep in, play, and read."

Mom nodded toward me. "Don't forget you have to practice piano every day, Matt."

I wish she'd forget.

John pointed at the VCR. "It's finished rewinding, Dad. You can hit 'play' now."

Dad held out the remote and punched a button. "Oh, Lisa, Fred Winters may stop by tomorrow."

"Thanks for letting me know."

"Quiet." John held a finger to his lips. "The movie's starting."

Luke fell asleep before the ship reached the Cliffs of Insanity. Dad lifted him from the sofa and held him, while Mom washed the orange coating off his fingers and from around his mouth. Dad carried Luke up the stairs, and Mom followed. I stretched out on the empty sofa and put the tan pillow under my head.

I'll stay up and see 1996 come in. Then it will be the year of the Camporee.

The next thing I knew, I woke with the sun shining through the patio door and in my eyes.

BANISHED

I washed my toy soldiers in the bathroom sink because I'd played outside with the little green guys. I shaped suds into snow banks, and pretended they hunkered under attack from Germans in World War II.

Mom stuck her head in. "Matt, why don't you go outside with John." She didn't say it with a question mark and she didn't wait for an answer. She held a book in one hand and gripped Luke's hand in the other.

Luke held up his Transformer backpack. "Look. My special things."

Mr. Winters must have come to our back door again.

Visitors usually rang the front doorbell, but he'd rung the back one four days in a row. He sat at the kitchen table with Dad, reading the Bible and asking questions.

The first three times, John and I were in our rooms, reading. But today, we were banished outside because of what happened the day before. While Dad and Mr. Winters were praying, John had dashed down the steps singing a rock song at the top of his lungs. To be fair, John hadn't known Mr. Winters was there. But now we both had to pay for his mistake.

As the drain sucked away the soapy water, I pulled an old towel from the closet.

Mom opened Dad's study door. "Fred Winters to see you, Tim."

Then she and Luke went upstairs.

Dad hurried past, glancing in just long enough to say, "Play outside for a bit, will you, Matt?" I heard the question mark, but he didn't wait for an answer either.

I left the soldiers wrapped in the wet towel on the counter. The fallout from leaving them there would be less than if I didn't get outside right away. Mom hadn't been very patient lately.

To avoid the kitchen, I snuck through the den and out the sliding glass door. John scrunched in a chair with an open book on the patio table. Even though he wore a heavy sweater, he shivered and rubbed his arms.

My hooded sweatshirt had been warm enough earlier, when I played with my soldiers in the melting snow caves. But it was colder now, and windier. Dark clouds raced across the sky like ships with full cargos of snow sailing on a gray sea.

John scowled at me. "Why can't that old Mr. Winters come to the front door like everybody else and talk to Dad in the study?"

"Beats me." I shrugged. "Whatcha reading?"

"*Out of the Silent Planet*." He blew on his hands.

"Part of the Space Trilogy by C. S. Lewis?"

"Yeah." He tilted his head. "How'd you know that?"

"Adam's been telling me about some C. S. Lewis stuff. Is that your own book?"

"Not exactly. I sort of borrowed it."

I was pretty sure he'd "borrowed" it from Dad's study, but I wasn't going to ask. For one thing, I didn't want him to know that I'd "borrowed" a book, too. Besides, I was trying to get along better with him. "How 'bout shooting some hoops? That'll warm us up."

John gazed at me as if I were a Dorito he was about to devour. "Let's play Pig." He left his book on the table while he got the basketball out of the garage.

I knew who'd be "Pig" first. I called after him, "Let's at least make it Horse."

He came out of the garage in a crouch, dribbling with fingers that covered half the ball, and was in the air for a layup before I saw it coming. The ball bounced off the backboard with a gentle thump and swooshed through the net.

He grinned, caught the ball, and fired it at me. "Didn't even touch the rim."

My hands stung as they stopped the missile, but I pretended not to notice.

My layup lacked John's style and the ball bumped the rim, but it went in. I faced away from the hoop and shot backward over my head. Amazingly, the ball swished through the basket.

John didn't say a thing. He dribbled to where I'd stood. Arching his back, he tossed the ball over his head, but it sailed over the board.

I danced a victory jig. "H!"

When I tried the same shot, the ball brushed the bottom of the net.

John grabbed the rebound and dribbled to where the three-point line would be. He aimed. "What do you think the deal is with that old Mr. Winters anyway?"

"No clue. Why doesn't Dad just ask him to go to the study like everybody else?"

"It's a mystery to me."

My heart sank with John's long shot. I lined up and eyed the hoop.

John waved. "Hey, you need to go back." He pointed. "At least another three feet."

I shuffled backward, keeping my eyes on the hoop. My shot came within a foot, but it was a definite miss.

"Close, but no cigar. H." John picked up the ball and dribbled around me. "Did you see what Mom was doing today when he knocked?"

"No, what?"

"Baking cookies with Luke standing on a chair beside her. I was in the living room, trying to read, while they were chanting—'cream together shortening and sugars'— then Mr. Winters knocks and she says, 'Oh, hello, Fred!' like he's her best friend. 'Come right in and have a seat while I get Tim.'"

John quoted Mom in a high voice that didn't sound anything like her. He kept talking while he dribbled around me and eyed the basket. "Then she grabs a book, pulls out Luke's backpack, tells me to get outta there, and scrams, leaving her mess all over the counter."

"She was holding a book about theology."

"Oh, no." John groaned. "This could be a while."

"Yeah, and she gave Luke his Transformer backpack."

If something was baking or supper was cooking, Mom would sit in a kitchen chair and read a little bit from a novel. But if Luke was taking a nap and we were staying out of her way, she'd sit in her recliner and read a book on theology.

Luke's Transformers backpack was stuffed with books, puzzles, and toys. Mom only let him have it when she wanted him to entertain himself quietly for a long time. She joked that the backpack "transformed" him into an "independent child."

John went in for a left-handed layup. He missed. He snagged the rebound and bent over, dribbling in short, fast bounces. Suddenly he leaped and flipped the ball through the net.

"Yes!" He punched the air. He hadn't even aimed.

"Hey, ball hog!" I yelled. "What about me? You forget someone else is playing here?"

We played hard without talking. I tried to retake the lead, but ended up mostly following his shots and slowly racking up letters.

"E! H-O-R-S-E." John punched my shoulder. "You're the horse, bro."

"You weren't that far behind me."

"Close only counts in horseshoes and hand grenades." John looked toward the kitchen window. "I hope old Mr. Winters is about ready to leave." He looked up and held out a hand. "Great. It's sprinkling. Let's go in. Nobody can get mad at us for coming in out of the rain."

We jogged around the garage, and John fired the ball into the open side door. He grabbed his book off the table. We opened the slider and crept into the den.

Dad and Mr. Winters sat at the kitchen table, looking at Dad's open study Bible.

We left the den light off and sat on the floor in front of the sofa. John opened his book. I found the latest *World* magazine and flipped to the political cartoon page.

Mr. Winters said, "I've been reading a chapter every day in the book of John, just like you told me, Pastor Tim, but there's a lot I don't understand."

"That's okay, Fred," Dad said. "What have you gotten out of it so far?"

"Well, the other day I read that God loved the world and gave his only Son."

"Do you know why God did that?"

"So anyone who believes in him can have eternal life."

"That's right."

"To be honest, Pastor Tim, I don't think I wanna live forever."

I stared at the man. Didn't he want to go to heaven?

Dad glanced at us and cleared this throat. "What are some things you don't understand?"

"Actually, most of it. I've never really read the Bible and I just don't get it. It all seems so complicated."

Dad stood up. "Come on." He pushed in his chair. "There's a book in my study I want you to borrow, *Mere Christianity* by C. S. Lewis."

I sucked in my breath. C. S. Lewis was the guy who wrote the Chronicles of Narnia. What if Dad saw the empty space? I looked at John. His eyes were wide.

Then he relaxed and grinned. He spoke quietly, like he was talking to himself. "Dad keeps theology books on the shelves behind his desk, separate from the fiction."

We laid low in the den until they came out a few minutes later.

"Thanks a lot, Pastor Tim." Mr. Winters shook Dad's hand. "Looks like I can handle this. It's a pretty small book."

"I think it will answer some questions, Fred. But call or stop in if you want to talk."

"Thanks. I guess I'd better get going." Mr. Winters turned at the door and looked into the den, right at us. "And let your mom finish her baking."

As soon as he closed the door, John snapped shut his book. "Hey, Dad, why can't Mr. Winters come to the front door like everybody else?"

Dad walked to the steps and called Mom and Luke before he turned to John. "He prefers to come and go quietly through the back door."

"I don't think he needs to disrupt the whole household every time he visits. If he's going to talk about personal stuff, why can't he go to the study?"

Dad picked up his Bible. "He feels more comfortable in the kitchen." He faced John. "Mr. Winters is welcome to come and go from whatever door he pleases and sit wherever he wants. And I'll thank you not to complain about it." He went into his study and shut the door.

John headed up the steps, grumbling. He pushed past Mom and Luke at the top.

Remembering my soldiers, I rushed to the bathroom. Mom would not be happy if she found that damp towel on the counter. I dumped the green guys into their shoebox and hung the towel on the shower rack.

Mom started the mixer in the kitchen. As I walked toward the steps, the back doorbell rang so I answered it.

It was Mr. Winters. I was so surprised that I didn't even say 'hello.'

He grinned and held up one of my soldiers. "Does this belong to you? I saw it lying on the driveway and I was afraid a car might ride over it."

"Yep, it's mine." I reached for it. "Thanks."

"No problem. You like soldiers, huh?"

"Guess so."

"I kinda do, too."

I couldn't think of what to say. We both stood there, not saying anything.

"Well, I better go." He turned away. "See you later."

"Yeah, see you later."

Through the door window, I watched him walk down the drive. The wind swung his ponytail to the side. The letters above the big badge on the back of his jacket said, "A-R-M-Y."

NOT A FUN DAY

Soldiers shouted at me from the trench. "Get down! Get down!" More shouts. "Get down here right now!"

I ducked behind a pile of sandbags and fell face-first into soft mud. A shell crashed nearby and a heavy timber slammed across my back. Trapped! I couldn't breathe.

I opened my eyes and realized I was in bed with my face pressed into my pillow. Luke had flung his arm across me. And Mom was yelling.

"Matthew Henry Vos, I told you to get down here right now!"

As soon as I came into the kitchen, I complained. "Can't you ever let me sleep in on Saturday, Mom?"

"I need your help." Mom opened the desk drawer and pawed through it. "Dad's at a pastor's conference. John's out of town for a game. Tomorrow your class will be trooping through here again, so we've got to clean. And I'm just not feeling very well."

Why did she still feel ill? Aunt Pam had been sick for a long time, too.

"As if that isn't enough, no one has agreed to be the helper for my Sunday school class." She shoved the drawer shut. "I have to phone some people this morning. I really do need your help today, Matt."

"Can I at least have breakfast first?"

"*May* I." Mom frowned. "Help yourself to some cereal, okay? I've got to find the church directory so I can make a list of names and telephone numbers."

I opened the cabinet and looked at the cereal choices. Maybe if Mom was this busy she'd forget about my piano lesson.

"Dad might have that directory in his office." She walked down the hall. "We need to finish cleaning in good time because I have to bake pies to take to the DeWitts' tonight. And remember to practice before your lesson this afternoon."

So much for her forgetting about that.

While I poured milk on my cereal, Luke stumbled down the steps. He came into the kitchen, rubbing his eyes. "I want some Cheerios."

"Help yourself." My cereal would turn soggy if I took time to get his ready for him.

"Just give him a hand, Matt," Mom called from the study. "It will save a lot of trouble, trust me."

I groaned and stood up. There were no more bowls in the cabinet, but I found one in the dishwasher. I think it was clean. I pulled the cereal box from the shelf, got out the milk, and filled the bowl. By the time he was happily munching his Cheerios, my Wheaties were mush.

While we ate, Mom sat at the kitchen table, looking in the directory and writing down names and phone numbers. Her glasses kept slipping down her nose and she'd push them back up with one finger. When she finished her list, she glanced at the clock. "It's still too early to make these calls." She gave me one of her no-nonsense looks. "You can help me clean first."

I wrinkled my nose. "Fun, fun."

"It could be," Mom said, "if you'd have the right attitude. Hurry and get dressed."

I dusted the living room while Mom vacuumed. She shut it off and sat down three times to rest, which was not at all like her. She was usually a cleaning tornado.

After we finished the living room, Mom began calling people. I sat on the sofa to watch cartoons with Luke.

"Matt." Mom punched in a number. "Dust the study."

"Why?" I didn't move. "We can just shut the door tomorrow, and no one will see it."

"If Dad has visitors next week, I don't want them to be able to write their names in the dust on his desk."

I found the feather duster and brushed it over Dad's desk and shelves.

Back in the kitchen, Mom chatted on the phone again. Luke sat like a zombie in front of "Animaniacs," so I watched it with him.

Mom smacked the cordless phone back into its holder. "Matthew Henry Vos." She frowned. "Can't you do more to help me?"

"I dusted Dad's study."

"What about dusting the bedrooms?"

"But Mom, 'Animaniacs' is on."

"You can at least do the furniture in the den while you're watching it."

I picked up the feather duster and swished it over the coffee table during commercials.

When "Animaniacs" was over, Mom sent me upstairs.

I ran the feather duster across the top of Mom and Dad's dresser. Then I went into John's room and brushed over his dresser and desk. His yearbook lay open on his bed. I picked it up.

It showed pictures of his classmates, including the identical twins, Rachel and Rebekah. I looked carefully at their pictures. They looked exactly the same to me, but John always called each one by her own name. How did he manage to tell them apart?

I walked down the hall toward my room. I wondered which Howard twin John liked best. He talked to both of them all the time.

I'd been reading a library book on World War I pilot aces the night before, when Mom poked her head in and made me go to bed. Now I flipped through the pages and read how the Red Baron was finally shot down. No one ever knew if the bullet was shot by Captain Brown, flying for the RAF, or Australian troops firing machine guns from the ground.

"Matt, come down for lunch."

Lunch? Where did the time go?

Flour covered the counter and unbaked pies sat on the stove. Mom spread peanut butter on bread.

I opened the fridge. "Can I get out jelly for PB&Js?"

"You *may* get out jelly and you *may* make peanut butter and jelly sandwiches."

Luke and I ate our sandwiches and drank milk. Mom nibbled on crackers.

When we finished eating, Mom got the Bible off the desk. Our family reads through the Bible for family devotions, a chapter or so at a time.

"We're in 1 Kings 18." Mom ran her finger down the page. "Remember we read last time that King Ahab and

Jezebel wanted to kill Elijah. We're ready for verse sixteen, 'Elijah on Mount Carmel.'"

I'd heard the story before, but it was one of my favorites. Elijah had a contest with the prophets of Baal. The people agreed that whichever god sent fire to an altar was the real God. Baal's prophets yelled all day. They even danced around and cut themselves, but no fire. No surprise. Elijah set up stones for an altar and dug a big trench around it. He had men pour water all over the altar three times until water filled the trench.

Then Elijah prayed, asking God to show that he is God. Fire fell from heaven and burned up the sacrifice, the wood, the stones, and the dirt. It even licked up the water in the trench.

When Mom finished, I sighed. "I love that story."

Luke's face was smeared with jelly. "I like it, too."

"It's a good reminder of God's power." Mom closed the Bible. "He can do anything."

After prayer, I put my empty glass in the dishwasher. "Mom, can we go to the library this afternoon? I want to get another book by Sigmund Brouwer."

"No, you *may* not go to the library today." Mom frowned. "You need to practice piano before your lesson—for a full hour."

"An hour! But I only have to practice for a half hour."

"That's if you do it every day; however, I know for a fact you have not practiced for at least two days, maybe more. I should make you do it for an hour and a half, but since you have your lesson today, I'll let you get by with just an hour."

"Thanks a lot."

"Don't get smart with me, young man."

I took my books from the denim bag I used for lessons and put them on the piano.

Mom brought her kitchen timer into the living room. She turned the dial to sixty minutes and set it beside the piano's keys. "An entire hour." She walked out. "But not too loud. I've got a few more calls to make."

I sighed. I opened my exercise book and began going through scales. It was so boring.

I made up a little song to go with the scales: *I want to go to Camporee. I hope Adam can go with me. I hope we're old enough to go. I cannot wait until we know.*

When I finished those exercises, I went through all the assigned songs in my other books twice. I looked at the timer. Still twenty-five minutes left.

I sighed. Then started in again on the scales.

I want to go to Camporee. I hope Adam can go with me. I hope we're old enough to go. I cannot wait until we know.

FRIENDS AND ENEMIES

Mom came into the living room, pulling on her jacket. "Matt, I can't get a helper and I'm running out of time for doing the craft. I'm going to pick up some supplies from Dollar General. I stuck the Clifford video in the player for Luke. Will you keep an eye on him while I'm gone?"

"Sure." Maybe I'd miss my piano lesson.

"I'll be back before you go to Mrs. Miller's."

Great.

As soon as she was out the door, I shut off the timer. I packed my books into the bag. Then I went into the den to watch the video with Luke.

My lesson was at 3:00, but Mom was back by 2:45.

I jumped up. "Did you get what you need?"

"I think so." She pulled things from a bag. "I picked up construction paper, Popsicle sticks, and Elmer's glue sticks. Maybe you can help me get the craft ready."

"Sounds like fun. I'd like to help."

Mom glanced at the clock. "Later. You have to leave now for your lesson, and I need to get those pies in the oven and clean up the kitchen."

I sighed and put on my coat. Then I got my bag from the living room. I put the strap over my shoulder. "I guess I'll be going now."

"Okay, Matt. Have a good lesson."

"I could stay home and help you with the craft stuff—"

"That's not necessary. Go to Mrs. Miller's. Now."

I unlocked the front door. I looked next door at Jenny's house. Brutus wasn't on the front porch. I sighed with relief and started down the front walk.

The Bergmans' front door flew open and Brutus lunged through, dragging Jenny behind him. I was glad to see she had both hands on his leash.

"Hi, Matt." Jenny lifted a hand and waved.

Oh, no! She shouldn't have done that!

Brutus leaped off the porch like King Kong jumping down from a skyscraper. He lunged toward me. I covered my face.

"Down, Brutus! Down! Bad dog!" Jenny yelled while Brutus stood with his front paws on my shoulders, slobbering all over my hands.

Jenny finally hauled him down and he stood in front of me, drooling on my shoes.

"Sorry about that," Jenny said cheerfully. "He sure likes you."

"I wish he didn't like me quite so much."

"You should be glad." Jenny grinned. "Better spit than teeth."

Brutus panted, his massive tongue hanging over his wolf teeth.

"Has he ever bitten anyone?"

"Not yet." She giggled. "But he growls something awful at John."

"He does?"

"Yeah, I don't know why. Whenever John talks to me, Brutus acts like he wants to take a chunk out of him."

Maybe that was why John called those two "Beauty and the Beast."

"Well, Brutus needs some exercise." Jenny pulled the monster away from me. "He tripped Mom when she was working in the kitchen, so I'm supposed to walk him for at least a half hour."

"Too bad."

"At least it's not snowing or raining." She smiled widely. John always said Jenny could look on the bright side of a train wreck. "I think I'll run over to the playground with him."

"Good idea." I inched down the sidewalk. "Find some little kids to terrorize."

"Ha, ha!" She laughed. "You Vos guys are hilarious."

She started jogging, but Brutus dashed ahead of her and stretched the leash tight. Jenny's legs turned like an airplane propeller. She looked about to become airborne.

I walked down the block and turned the corner.

"Hey, PK-2!"

It was Josh. He always called me that. "PK" stands for "Preacher's Kid" and "2" is because I'm the second kid in the family. He used to call John "PK-1," until John punched him in the nose and made it bleed all over his new Hawkeye hooded sweatshirt. Now he doesn't call John anything. In fact, he goes out of his way to avoid him. What's most amazing is that John never got into trouble over it. We were playing basketball, and Josh told his mom that a fast pass smacked him in the face. And she believed him. She never even mentioned it to our parents. John never mentioned it either.

Josh yelled again. "Hey, PK-2!"

Maybe if I ignore him, he'll go away. I kept walking.

"Hey, Matt." Josh stood in front of me. "What've you got in that snazzy bag?"

"Just my piano lesson books."

"Piano lessons? You take piano lessons?"

"Yeah."

"Oh, man. I thought only girls took piano lessons."

I reminded myself that Christians are supposed to love their enemies.

"My sister always gets a new dress for her recitals." Josh walked backward in front of me. "Do you get a new dress for your recital?"

If God made fire fall from heaven on Mount Carmel, couldn't he make Josh trip?

I took a deep breath. *Lord, forgive me for thinking that and help me to love—or at least not to hate—my enemies. And my so-called friends.*

Josh stuck his face in mine. "You headed to lessons now, PK-2?"

If he wants to talk to me, he can use my right name. I walked faster.

Josh turned and walked beside me. "Come on, Matt." He slapped my shoulder. "Lighten up. I was just teasing."

"I didn't think it was funny."

We reached Mrs. Miller's house and I walked to her front door. I rang the bell, looking out the corner of my eye to where Josh still stood on the sidewalk.

Usually I hope Mrs. Miller won't answer the door and I can go home, but that time I really hoped she'd answer—and fast.

She finally opened the door. "Hello, Matthew. Right on time as usual."

"Hi, Mrs. Miller. Can—may I wash my hands?"

She blinked. "Why certainly. Come this way."

She opened the door to a bathroom, and I washed my hands with a flower-shaped soap that smelled like the perfume Mom hardly ever wears.

Mrs. Miller waited in the hall. After I dried my hands on a towel with a stiff flower on it, I followed her into the dim living room. Thin white curtains hung over the front window. A baby grand piano took up most of the space. The rest was crowded with tables and shelves full of glass stuff. I always held my breath when I walked through Mrs. Miller's living room maze because I was afraid I'd bump into a table and break something valuable.

Her house was so quiet, I heard the big grandfather clock tick-tocking. I sat at the piano and tried to get my books out of the bag without rustling the pages.

Mrs. Miller sat straight in a kitchen chair beside the piano bench. She smiled like we were going to have fun. "Let's begin with our scales."

If they're "our" scales, you could do them for once.

I pressed the pages so the book would stay open. Then I began running through this lesson's scale exercises.

"Not so fast, Matthew. Take your time to do it right."

Just like Mr. Rogers.

After I played my assigned songs, Mrs. Miller made me play the next song in each book. She kept stopping me and telling me things I needed to do differently.

"Take those songs for next week," she said, "and do— let's see—the next five scale exercises in this book."

"Okay." I shoved one book into my bag.

"You know, Matthew, you would do better if you'd practice more often." Mrs. Miller tapped a pink fingernail on the piano. "I really believe you have natural talent and I know you love music. I've noticed how much you enjoy singing during the worship services at church."

Without thinking, I blurted, "But hymns are so much better than boring old scales."

Mrs. Miller's eyes widened and her eyebrows went so high they hid under her curly gray bangs. "I know scales can be boring, but they help us become accomplished pianists." She stood and moved her chair against the wall. "Run through the scale exercises and your assigned songs at least twice when you practice. You should spend a minimum of a half hour at it each day."

"Each day?" I shoved another book in my bag. "Even Sunday?"

"You don't have to practice on Sunday," Mrs. Miller said quickly, "unless your parents ask you to."

As I put the last book in my bag, I tried to see if Josh was still on the sidewalk outside. But I didn't see his silhouette through the thin curtains.

At Mrs. Miller's front door, I took a deep breath. I opened it a crack and peeked out.

No Josh to the left. No Josh to the right.

Stand up, sit down, fight, fight, fight, I added, remembering a basketball cheer.

I chanted the cheer as I ran down the sidewalk. *No Josh to the left. No Josh to the right. Stand up, sit down, fight, fight, fight.*

I heard an engine noise and looked up to see an airplane flying low overhead.

I pretended it was the Red Baron's red triplane and I was Captain Brown. The Red Baron was after my buddy, Lieutenant May, whose guns had jammed and who was trying to get back to base. I swerved my plane to follow the Red Baron. I had him in my sights. I was closing fast. I aimed and squeezed the gun trigger—BAM!

13

DOWN AND FINALLY OUT

What happened? I didn't know the forecast was for a slime storm.

I lay flat on my back on the cold sidewalk, trying to focus through a film of slime. My head hurt. I felt like I'd been hit by a cement truck. And it was still on top of me. Then I smelled something familiar—Brutus breath.

Jenny's voice was far away. "Brutus, you bad old dog!"

Her voice came nearer. "Let him up right now. Let him up, I say!"

The truck drove off my chest. I sat up, rubbing the goose egg bump on the back of my head and blinking dog slobber out of my eyes.

"Here." Jenny pressed something soft into my hand. "You could use a tissue."

I wiped one eye and the tissue was soaked. Jenny handed me another. All together it took six to dry my face. Good thing she had a full pocket pack with her.

I handed her the last slimy tissue. "Have you ever thought about giving him less water?"

"Ha, Ha!" Jenny laughed. "You are so funny. Let me help you up."

"No, thanks." I quickly waved her away. "Keep both hands on that leash."

"Yes, sir."

"Sorry. I just think you should keep King Kong under control."

"Right." Jenny giggled. "Well, we've put in our outdoor time, so Kong and I are ready to head home."

"Good idea."

"See you later."

"Not if I can help it," I said under my breath.

I walked home slowly, rubbing the back of my head.

When I came through the front door, the oven timer was buzzing, the phone was ringing, and Luke was screaming. Mom ran up the basement stairs with a basket of laundry in her arms.

"Get the phone," she yelled.

I ran to pick up the phone while she shut off the buzzer. Then she pulled Luke into the bathroom and shut the door.

"Hello, Vos residence," I said. "Matthew speaking."

"Matt." It was Adam. "Just who I wanted to talk to."

"Hi, Adam." I ran my hand over the bump on the back of my head. It was only about as big as a robin egg now.

"Hey, have you finished reading *The Lion, the Witch and the Wardrobe* yet?"

"Not yet."

"It's just a short book. It can't possibly take you this long to read. I know what—bring it over this evening. Maybe you can finish reading after dinner and we can talk about it."

"I don't think that's going to work."

"Why not?"

"I'd love to chat, Adam, but Mom really needs my help right now."

"She does?"

"Yes, she does. I'll talk to you tonight, okay?"

"Okay. See you later."

Mom and Luke came back into the kitchen. Luke held up a finger with a Superman Band-Aid on it.

I looked at Mom. "What happened?"

"He dropped the toy box lid on his finger." Mom pushed hair out of her face. "Who was on the phone?"

"It was Adam. He just wanted to talk, but I told him I needed to help you."

John ran through the back door and slammed it behind him. "We won by twelve points." He pumped his fist. "And I sunk six of them."

"That's great, John." Mom frowned at him. "But don't slam the door."

The back door opened again, and Dad walked in. "Hi, honey." He kissed Mom. "How are you feeling? How was your day?"

"I need to take the foil off the edges of the pies right now." She pushed Luke toward him. "And Luke needs some ice on his finger to keep it from swelling."

"Don't worry." Dad took Luke's arm. "I'll see to that."

Mom opened the oven and glanced up. "Get in the shower, John. We need to leave soon for the DeWitts'."

I touched the back of my head. The bump felt as small as a wren's egg. No need to mention it to Mom. I went upstairs and stretched out on my bed. I stared at the ceiling. What was I going to do about Mom's book?

John walked past my door to his room. Should I ask him about Mom's book? Maybe he'd have an idea for how to get it out of Mr. Harding's Black Hole.

I walked down the hall to his open door. He yanked clean underwear out of his drawer. I knocked on the door frame. "Hey."

John jumped and turned his head. "Hey, yourself." He opened his sock drawer. "What do you want?"

"I want to talk to you."

"I don't have time to talk." He shook his head. "I have to get in the shower right now."

"It won't take long."

"Mom will have my hide if I don't get in the shower right away. She's already upset with me for eating the last of the fudge and slamming doors."

"She hasn't been very patient lately."

"That's for sure. She's been downright crabby." John glared at me. "But don't tell her I said that."

"I won't."

"Promise?"

"I promise."

"How do I know I can trust you? You've been the world's biggest tattler lately."

"I promised I won't tell her and I won't."

"Okay." John grabbed clean jeans and headed for the door. "You can leave my room now."

I followed him into the hall.

"You know, that could be *our* room—"

"No way. Even if I had a room big enough for two beds, I wouldn't want to share it with you." He started down the stairs and I followed him.

"Why not?"

"Because you're always getting me into trouble."

"Not anymore."

"Look." John stopped at the bottom of the steps. "There's no way it would work for you to share my room. It's too small, and my bed is only big enough for one person—me." He dashed into the bathroom and shut the door.

"Matt," Dad said. "Give it a rest. John's right, you know—it just won't work for you to share his room."

"But I hate sharing a room with Luke."

"Watch what you say, Matt." Mom frowned. "Think how that makes Luke feel."

Luke sat at the table, drinking a glass of milk with one hand, while Dad held an ice pack on the injured finger of his other hand.

"That makes me feel real bad." Luke wiped his milky mouth with his sleeve. "Can I have a cookie?"

"No, you may not," Mom said. "I want you to eat all your food when we have dinner at the DeWitts' tonight."

What would I tell Adam when he asked why I didn't bring the book?

Turned out Adam never asked about the book because after dinner we split into family teams and played Pictionary. We had fun, even though the DeWitts won most of the games. They were either more artistic than our family or they knew each other better since they homeschooled and spent so much time together.

We got home late, but Mom let me stay up even later to help get the craft ready for her Sunday school class.

We cut out little ships from brown construction paper and little Peter figures from white. We cut slits in the boats and in sheets of blue construction paper. The kids were supposed to glue the boats to the sheets of blue construction paper and glue the Peter figures to Popsicle sticks. Then they could put Peter in and out of the boat when he tried to walk across the water toward Jesus.

When we finally finished all that work, Mom looked at the clock.

"Oh, my." She gave me a gentle shove. "You've got to get to bed right now. It's 10:48."

I yawned and walked upstairs. I put on my pajamas, pushed Luke over, and crawled in beside him. But I didn't even remember dropping my head on the pillow.

14

TROUBLE WITH A CAPITAL T

I was having a weird dream about being a pig with an apple stuffed in my mouth, when I woke up to discover something *was* in my mouth. Luke's elbow.

I spat it out and pushed away his arm. I was glad he'd at least had a bath the night before.

That reminded me I needed to shower. On my way downstairs, I heard Dad talking in the kitchen. "They seem to be getting along better the last couple of days. What do you think?"

"I think they're trying," Mom answered. "And it will probably improve more when they go back to school tomorrow and don't see so much of each other."

They're talking about John and me. I stopped and held my breath.

"Maybe that's been most of the problem," Dad said. "Too much togetherness."

I waited a little longer, but no one said anything else, so I jumped on the squeaky third step and then went all the way down and into the kitchen. Mom closed the oven. Dad put a lid on a pan on the stove.

"Whatcha making, Dad?"

"Oatmeal."

"That's what I was afraid of."

"It's a good breakfast for a winter morning. Sticks to your ribs." Dad rubbed my side with his knuckles. It tickled, and I giggled.

He put a trivet on the table "You're up early."

"Good thing," Mom said. "He has to shower."

"But breakfast is ready." Dad set the pan on the table. "We ought to get the other boys up."

"I thought John was—" I clamped my lips shut.

"—going to set his alarm?" Mom washed her hands at the sink. "I thought so, too."

At that very moment, an alarm went off upstairs.

"I'll go wake Luke." Dad started up the stairs. "And make sure John is getting up."

He headed upstairs, and I went to the bathroom.

When I came back into the kitchen, Mom opened a box of saltines.

I frowned. "Is that what you're having for breakfast?"

"It is today."

Luke shuffled down the steps, and Dad walked calmly behind him. We were all sitting at the table when John thumped down and dropped onto his chair. His hair stuck up in greasy clumps and his eyes were two red slits.

He scowled. "Why do we have to get up so early on Sundays?"

"I have to go over to church soon." Dad plopped a glob of oatmeal into Luke's bowl. "I'm meeting with the parents of two babies being baptized this morning."

"Fine. Why don't you just go and the rest of us can eat breakfast later?"

"Because we're going to have breakfast and devotions together, that's why."

"We'll have devotions together at noon and again this evening." John's eyes were wide open now. "We only have them twice on school days, and today we'll read the Bible and pray during two services. It wouldn't kill us to miss breakfast devotions."

"You can never have too many devotions." Dad folded his hands. "Shall we pray?"

I closed my eyes, but immediately opened them because John kept talking. "Mom always leads devotions when you're gone. She could do them later."

"I said, 'Shall we pray.'" Dad glared at John before dropping his head and rushing into prayer. He asked God to bless our food and to help us respect authority.

After breakfast, Mom stood. "John and Matt, you both need to shower."

"You first." John nudged past as we walked upstairs. "I want to finish some reading."

I couldn't get my shower very warm. As I lathered the shampoo in my hair, the water turned completely cold. I shut off the faucets and hollered.

Wouldn't you know I had forgotten to lock the door? Mom waltzed right in and opened the shower curtain. She made me rinse out the shampoo with ice-cold water, but at least I got her to leave the room first.

I dressed and came out of the bathroom, shivering. I tapped Mom's arm. "Do my lips look blue?"

She glanced at me, but didn't have a chance to answer before John came up from the basement.

"The water heater has apparently sprung a leak. A pool of water is spreading around it even as we speak."

Mom sighed and put a hand on her forehead. "At least it's near the drain. Maybe most of the water will go down before it reaches the carpet." She looked at John. "You'll have to skip your shower this morning. Get dressed."

John stared at Mom. "You can't be serious. I'm not going to church without showering. My hair is gross. I'll just stay home."

"Oh, no, you won't. People used to bathe only once a week. You can get by for one day."

"Well, people used to stink, didn't they? I'm not going anywhere unless I shower first."

They argued for a bit, but they finally compromised. Mom put water in the teakettle on the stove so John could have warm water to wash his hair and armpits. He bent his head over the kitchen sink, and she lathered shampoo in his hair. While she was doing that, she sent me to the attic to find a flat box for carrying her Sunday school craft stuff to church.

At Christmas, Mom had given Dad a shirt in a white box. Where was it? I moved the tub of tree ornaments and pawed past the rolls of wrapping paper. I finally found that flat white box. When I came back with it, Mom was rinsing John's head with water from the kettle.

Luke hopped into the kitchen. Like the little boy in the nursery rhyme, he had one shoe off and one shoe on. "I can't find my other shoe."

Mom glanced up. "Did you look in your closet?"

"Yes."

"Did you look under your bed?"

"Yes."

"Look again."

He hopped back upstairs.

Mom suddenly set down the teakettle and leaned on the counter.

I touched her shoulder. "You okay?"

Little drops of sweat beaded on her forehead. She grabbed a kitchen towel and wiped her face—something she'd never let me get by with. "Maybe I'm a little nervous about teaching Sunday school." She swallowed. "Maybe this extra stress is making it worse."

"Hey." John still bent over the sink. "I'm standing here with shampoo in my hair."

"Finish rinsing yourself." I slapped the box on the table. "Maybe you wouldn't think Mom was so crabby if you weren't always giving her such a hard time."

Mom looked up. "What?"

"Why you little—" John jerked up his soapy head. Suds smacked the window and ran down the glass, leaving glistening streaks like snail trails.

"John, keep your head down." Mom pushed it down for him. "Matt's right—about rinsing your own hair anyway, you can handle that."

She turned to me. "Matt, go upstairs and see if you can help Luke find that other shoe."

As I went up the stairs, Mom asked, "Now what's all this about me being crabby?"

John is going to kill me.

Luke sat in the middle of the bed, staring at the one shoe on his one foot.

We looked through all the shoes in the closet. We looked under the bed. We looked behind our desks. I picked up Luke's pajamas from the floor—with one finger, I even picked up his underwear—but we couldn't find the shoe.

We went downstairs. John was drying his hair in the bathroom with the door shut.

"No shoe," I reported to Mom.

She piled her teacher's manual, a pack of student papers, and the flat craft box on her Bible. She sighed.

Luke hopped around, singing, "My shoe is lost. My shoe is lost."

"Oh, hush, Luke." Mom grabbed his hand and pulled him up the steps. I followed. I didn't want to be alone in the kitchen when John came out of the bathroom.

Lord, please keep John from killing me.

Our bed wasn't made yet, so Mom jerked the covers over the pillows. But they came loose and flew in the air. She sighed and started tucking them back in. As she was smoothing the covers on Luke's side of the bed, she suddenly stopped. She reached down and pulled a shoe from between the mattress and the bed frame.

She grinned and held it up. "The lost is found."

I smiled. Luke stopped hopping.

A scary voice suddenly said, "I'd like a word with Matt." John stood at the door.

"No, you wouldn't." Mom held up one hand. "You don't have to talk to him about anything. It's probably all for the best. I realize now that I haven't been very patient lately and I'll try to do better. You don't need to discuss this any further with your brother."

John walked in and glared at me. A muscle on the side of his face twitched.

Mom steered him around. "Go to your own room and get ready for church, John."

He began walking out, but he suddenly stopped by my desk. "What in the world?" He snatched up a book and whirled toward me. "How did my school annual get on your desk?"

"Uh—" I looked at the book he held. It was the one with pictures of his classmates.

I am dead meat.

"I guess I was holding it when I dusted your room and brought it in here by accident."

"By accident, huh?" John came toward me. "I'll show you an accident."

"John." Mom blocked him with her hands on his chest. "That's quite enough. Go to your room. Now."

"Matt, take Luke over to church." She motioned us out. "John and I will be there soon."

15

MORE TROUBLE AND NO TROUBLE

Luke and I hurried downstairs and out the door. We walked across the sidewalk and through the parking lot, which was full of cars. Inside church, the pews were almost full, too. The DeWitts had already sat down. We stood at the back as latecomers trickled in.

John finally came through the door and up the steps.

I asked, "Where's Mom?"

He turned his back toward me and talked to Luke. "Tell your brother that Mom will be here soon. She's looking for crayons for Sunday school and can't find a box without any broken ones."

"Matt," said Luke, "Mom will be here soon. She's—"

"I heard, I heard."

Just then Mom walked up the steps. Her hair fell in front of her face. Her purse swung from her shoulder as she tried to balance her Bible, her book, student papers, and the craft box flat in front of her.

When she reached the top step, I couldn't believe my eyes. On her feet were her fluffy pink slippers.

I ran to her. "Mom," I whispered. "You're still wearing your slippers."

Mom held her stack off to the side and stared at her feet in horror. She shoved her stuff into my hands and ran back down the steps and out the door.

John's face was red. He grabbed Luke's hand. "C'mon, Luke. Let's sit down."

I looked at the pile in my hands. Then I ran to the basement and put it on the desk in the preschool room. I started up the steps, but remembered that Mom would want her Bible during church and ran back for it.

By the time I got upstairs, Mom was coming through the door again. She must have really hoofed it home and back. She took her Bible from me. "Where's my other stuff?"

"I put it on the desk in your classroom."

"Good. Thanks."

Dad and the elders and deacons came out of the room where they met. He stopped beside us. "You're just getting here now? What was the holdup?"

"Don't get me started." Mom's stressed face broke into a smile. "Good morning, Fred."

Sure enough, Mr. Winters was sneaking in behind us at the last minute.

"Morning." He held out a hand. "Hi, Pastor Tim."

"Fred." Dad shook his hand. "Have you had a chance to read any of that book yet?"

"Read the whole thing." Mr. Winters grinned. "And I've got more questions."

"I'll try to answer them." Dad glanced at his watch. "But I'd better get up front now. What about having lunch with us today?"

Mr. Winters smiled wider. "Sure."

"See you then." Dad walked down the center aisle.

Mom hurried toward the right aisle.

"Hey." Mr. Winters grabbed my arm. "Been playing soldier lately?"

"Uh—" I looked at Mom, who was already halfway down the aisle. "Sometimes." I hurried to catch up.

Mom climbed around John and pushed over Luke so she could sit between them. There was a little room between John and the outside of the pew, so I squeezed in and hugged the edge.

John whispered, "Trade places with me."

"No way," I whispered back.

Mom scowled at us.

I noticed the usher standing beside our pew. He held up a finger. I let go of the arm and pushed against John until he slid over. Mr. Winters sat beside me.

I read the activities listed on the back of the bulletin. Under "Wednesday," it said, "Cadets." I couldn't wait. We were sure to hear something about the Camporee.

Dad made some announcements before the service. He reminded the congregation that an adult Bible study class was beginning after morning worship.

When we stood to sing the first song, I had to share the hymnal with Mr. Winters. The song was "Stand Up, Stand Up for Jesus." I was really belting out, "Stand up, stand up for Jesus, Ye soldiers of the cross," but I couldn't hear Mr. Winters singing, so I toned it down.

I was excited for Dad to preach from Ephesians 6 because I wanted to hear about the spiritual armor. Turned out he hardly talked about armor at all. He said that our strength was not in ourselves, but only in God.

We sang "Christian, Do You See Them?" after the sermon. I sang softly at first because that's how the song starts out. I could hear Mr. Winters. By the time we got to the end of the last verse, we were both singing loudly: "Christian, answer boldly: 'While I breathe I pray!' Peace shall follow battle, night shall end in day."

As we walked up the aisle after the service, I asked him, "You coming for dinner?"

"If it's not too much trouble."

"It won't be. Mom makes plenty of food on Sundays because we're always inviting somebody over."

"Then I guess I'll be 'somebody' today."

"Okay, see you later." I grabbed my coat and met Adam at the door. As we walked to our class at my house, we talked about what fun we'd have this year at the Camporee. I just hoped we'd both be old enough to go.

16

PEACE FOLLOWS BATTLE

During catechism class, I sat squeezed between Adam and Angela on our living room sofa. She'd rolled her eyes when she saw she'd have to sit beside me. Every time the roast beef smell from the kitchen made my stomach growl, Angela scowled at me. But when Adam's stomach gurgled, she didn't even frown.

Finally Mr. Thomason dismissed the class. "Stay on the sidewalk on your way back. Except Matthew, of course—who doesn't even have to leave the house."

Everyone laughed. As they filed through the door, I ran upstairs to put on jeans and a sweatshirt. When I came down, Mr. Winters stood at the counter, slicing a steaming roast. Mom opened a jar of applesauce. Luke was setting silverware around, so I got out napkins.

Mom watched me fold one and slide it under a fork. "Do you have clean hands?"

"No." I turned on the faucet. "But I have a pure heart." The "pure heart" thing was from the Psalms and was our standard response to Mom's question.

John came in and stood with the refrigerator door open. "Can we have olives?"

"*May* we." Mom sighed. "Put some on a dish. But don't eat more than a few—they're loaded with sodium."

Luke looked up. "What's sodium?"

"Salt." Mom put the bowl of applesauce on the table. "Too much is bad for your heart."

"My Sunday school teacher says Jesus lives in my heart." Luke's eyes widened. "I don't want Jesus to get salty."

Dad walked in, smiling and rubbing his hands. "Hello, hello, hello. What a gorgeous day. Better enjoy it. Supposed to snow tomorrow. Nice job carving the roast, Fred. Couldn't have done better myself."

Dad put his arms around Mom and—in front of Mr. Winters and all of us—kissed her lips. "How'd class go?"

"Not bad," Mom said. "Some kids had trouble sitting still, and the Peter cutouts fell off the Popsicle sticks. I told the children to have their parents help them with it."

"Good call. How can I help?"

"The vegetables need to go in a bowl."

"I'm on it." Dad grabbed a slotted spoon and scooped potatoes, carrots, and onions from the roasting pan. "Say, Fred, what did you do during Sunday school?"

"I went to that new class you mentioned."

"Great. I'm glad you did." Dad put the bowl mounded with vegetables on the table. "What did you think?"

"Tom Loursma was easy to understand and didn't mind my questions." Mr. Winters put the platter of roast beef on the table. "Almost as good a teacher as you."

"Almost as good as me." Dad lifted Luke and swung him around. "How 'bout that, Luke?"

Luke shrieked. "My daddy's the best!"

"You got it, kiddo." Dad set him on his feet and rubbed his head. "Remember that when you're sixteen."

During the meal, we talked and laughed. Then Mr. Winters asked when we'd go back to school. We told him tomorrow, but we didn't laugh.

When he asked about sports, John told him every detail of his basketball game the day before.

Mr. Winters said over and over how much he appreciated a home-cooked meal.

After finishing off the Snicker bar salad, I was still hungry. "What's for dessert?"

"I baked apple pies yesterday." Mom collected plates. "Would you like some, Fred?"

"I'd love a piece, but I'm too stuffed." He frowned. "Guess I'll have to pass."

Dad crumpled his napkin and dropped it on his plate. "How about having pie later?"

Mr. Winters smiled. "Sounds good to me."

Dad looked at the rest of us. Luke and I nodded. John scooped the last strings of beef from his plate. "I could handle a piece of pie now." Dad stared at him until he glanced up. Then he looked down. "But I'll wait 'til later."

"That settles it." Dad opened the Bible at the bookmark. "I'll read from 1 Kings 19."

He read about how Elijah ran for his life because Jezebel planned to kill him. He wanted to lie down and die. But the angel of the Lord gave him food that made him strong enough to run for forty days and nights. He hid in a cave and had a pity party because he thought he was the only one left who served God. After a wind, an earthquake, and a fire, God spoke to Elijah in a whisper. He told him there were still seven thousand believers.

Dad closed the Bible. "Elijah thought he was all alone and felt like giving up. He thought his life was as good as over, but God still had work for him to do."

After prayer, we boys cleared the table. Mom filled the dirty pans with water.

Mr. Winters leaned his elbows on the table. "So what work did Elijah still have to do?"

"He anointed the next kings and the prophet who took over for him," Dad said. "When Elijah's work was finished, he didn't die."

"He didn't?"

"No. A fiery chariot and horses appeared. Then a whirlwind took him to heaven."

Mom shut the loaded dishwasher, but walked away without starting it.

Dad looked up absently. "Shouldn't you start the dishwasher?"

"Ah, I would, but—." She put her hand on his shoulder. "There's no hot water."

He twisted to look at her face. "Why not?"

"Because the water heater sprung a leak."

Dad jumped up. "We'd better call Ed. He chairs the building committee."

"No need. I didn't think we wanted to wait for a committee meeting. I caught Harold Loursma on my way to Sunday school and explained the problem to him."

Just then a vehicle pulled into our driveway. Through the kitchen window, I saw it was a Loursma Plumbing and Heating pickup with a big box in the back. Harold and Tom Loursma came to the back door.

Dad opened the door. "You know, we can wait until tomorrow if you don't want to do this today."

"Ach, Dominee," said old Mr. Loursma. "A water heater with a burst seam is like a cow in a pit. We can't leave it there just because it's Sunday. The Lord don't care if we do a little emergency work on his special day. Besides, Tom and me are doing this on our own time. We're not conducting business on the Sabbath, we're just helping out a brother."

"That's—that's wonderful, but you'll send a bill for the water heater, won't you?"

"Oh, now, don't you be worrying about that. The Lord's been good to me and Tom and we figure we can donate one little water heater to the church, especially when it's for our pastor's family."

Dad was at a loss for words, which didn't happen very often.

While the Loursmas installed the new water heater, Mr. Winters used their wet and dry vac to suck up pools of water from the bare floor and the carpet. He helped them load the old water heater and their vacuum, and then they left.

I found two fans in the storage area, and Mr. Winters set them up to blow on the wettest parts of the carpet.

Then he sat beside me on the basement steps. "Those fans will help keep the carpet from mildewing."

I nodded. "It sure didn't take the Loursmas long to put in that new water heater."

"Reckon they've done that sort of thing a time or two."

The fans whirred like locusts on a summer evening.

"Thanks for sharing your songbook with me." Mr. Winters rubbed his scruffy chin. "I had fun singing that one song with you."

"Me, too. I like the way it gets loud at the end."

"I liked that too. 'Peace shall follow battle, night shall end in day.'"

"Yeah, that's cool."

"I know you like soldiers, Matthew, and playing war. But pretend war isn't anything like real war."

"I know," I said quickly. "People can get hurt—even killed—in real war."

"Terrible things happen during a war." Mr. Winters cleared his throat. "It can be real tough. And sometimes the toughest part is after you come home."

I couldn't figure that out. "What do you mean?"

"I used to be a soldier. And I fought in a real war. Vietnam."

About all I knew about the Vietnam War was a picture in a library book that showed a naked child, screaming and running in front of a fire. I shuddered. "You fought in Vietnam? Wasn't that terrible?"

"It was." Mr. Winters spoke so quietly I barely heard him over the humming fans. "A lot of guys died. My best buddy lost both legs." He cupped his hands over his face. "I'll never forget when he stepped on that booby trap."

He rubbed his forehead with his fingers. "I was one of the lucky ones, I guess. I came back—all in one piece."

I gulped. "I'm glad you did."

"It hasn't been easy. Vietnam veterans weren't exactly popular when I got back. Once when some other vets and

I were in a parade, a group of college kids came up and yelled names at us and spat in our faces."

Mom doesn't even let us spit on the sidewalk.

Mr. Winters seemed to have forgotten I was there. He stared at a spinning fan blade. "It got harder and harder to keep going. I kept having dreams." He laughed in a weird way. "I stayed sane through all the garbage in 'Nam, and then got totally messed up when I was safe and sound, back in the good ole U S of A."

As Mr. Winters talked, I felt like he wasn't even speaking to me. "I married my high school sweetheart, but I couldn't seem to hold down a job. I started drinking to try to get rid of the dreams. It got to be more than she could handle, and she left me for another guy. After that, life pretty much stank."

He looked at me for a while as if he was trying to remember who I was. "Anyway, you should know that it's okay to be willing to fight for some things. It might even be okay to be willing to die for something. But you've got to be very careful about picking your battles."

The fans hummed.

"I think," I said, "serving God is worth dying for. Daniel was willing to be thrown to the lions. And his friends were tossed into the fiery furnace. Those guys knew bad things might happen to them, but they also knew it was more important to serve God."

Light from the basement bulb glinted in Mr. Winters's eyes. "I haven't heard those old stories in years."

"Oh, I hear them all the time." I waved a hand. "Dad says we don't know how every battle will end, but we do know that the final victory is the Lord's."

Mr. Winters grinned a little. "'Peace shall follow battle, night shall end in day,' right, Matt?"

"Right, Mr. Winters." I stood and stretched. "Let's go have some apple pie."

A VERY BAD MORNING

During the night, I heard Mom being sick again. I ran downstairs, but she wasn't in the bathroom. I looked in Dad's study, but she wasn't there. She wasn't in the den or the living room. I opened the basement door, but it was dark. I tried to yell, but my throat was paralyzed.

Then I woke up.

Outside the window, the streetlight shone on a blur of falling snowflakes. Beside me, Luke breathed through his mouth like a puppy with asthma.

All Christmas break, I'd tried to forget about Mom's lost book. Now I had to think of a way to retrieve it. Maybe I could discuss it privately with John. I slipped out of bed and crept into his room.

"Hey, John," I whispered. I didn't hear his breathing at all. I wished I shared his room.

I patted his lumpy bed, but the bumps were all soft. Not one of them was John.

A panicky feeling grew in my tummy. I hurried back to the door and fumbled for the light switch. The glaring light showed only a messed up, but empty bed. No John.

His clock said 6:58. He was probably already at practice. I dashed downstairs.

The kitchen light was on, but Mom wasn't there or in the den. The bathroom door was open, but she wasn't in there. I looked in Dad's study. The living room. I threw open the basement door, but gazed down into a dark pit.

My nightmare was coming true!

I ran up to my parents' room and flipped on the light. Mom sat up and blinked at me.

"Oh, my." She rubbed her eyes. "What time is it?"

Before I finished saying, "About 7:00," she'd thrown off the covers and put on her slippers. "Wake Luke and get dressed." She grabbed her robe. "I'll start breakfast."

The only times I'd ever seen Mom in bed were once when she'd had the flu and the day we visited her in the hospital after Luke was born.

By the time Luke and I ran down, Mom had milk and cereal in bowls and orange juice in glasses. I wouldn't have picked Total, but I figured complaining wouldn't do any good.

Luke wasn't eating fast enough for Mom, so she used another spoon to shove in more every time he swallowed. I ate as quickly as I could.

Mom and I kept glancing at the clock. The bus stopped in the next block at 7:20, and it would take a while to get there because Luke's so slow.

Mom dug out our snow boots and gloves. While we zipped our coats, she slipped our backpack straps over our shoulders. She shoved us out the door at 7:16.

"Walk fast." She closed the door against the snow. Then she opened it again. "God bless you. I love you."

"God bless you. Love you," we called back, but kept shuffling down the driveway. I pulled Luke along. "Come on, Luke Slow Walker. We've got a bus to catch."

When we turned the corner, I sighed with relief. The other kids were still at the stop. Dan and Mike tossed snowballs at a sign. Dan caught sight of me. "Hey, PK."

He and Mike ran over. Luke hurried to the little kids.

"Hey, Matt." Mike tossed a snowball up and caught it. "What'd you get for Christmas?"

"Just what I wanted." I grinned. "A break from you two."

"I got a BB gun." Mike tossed the snowball higher and caught it again. "My dad and I shot targets at the old rock quarry three times during Christmas vacation."

"I got a four-wheeler," Dan said. "My dad had the whole week off between Christmas and New Year's, so we went four-wheeling every day."

Behind me, a familiar voice sang, "What's new with you, PK-2?"

Like usual, I ignored Josh, but—as always—he got in my face. "Dad bought us a new Ping-Pong table. My brother's teaching me everything he knows. He's been the high school intramural champ for two years."

For Christmas I'd gotten *The Visual Dictionary of Special Military Forces*, which was in my backpack, and a Flexible Flyer sled that was still in the garage because Dad had been too busy to take me sledding.

The bus drove up and the little kids got on first, led by an annoying pair of giggling sisters. My assigned seat was beside Josh. As soon as I sat down, I took out my *Visual Dictionary* and pretended to read so I didn't get asked again about presents. And so I could think.

How can I get Mom's book out of the Black Hole? Should I try to talk to Mr. Harding? I wish I'd had a chance to ask John about it this morning.

After we got off the bus at school, I walked into the front hall and stopped. The office door was as big as a castle gate. It looked as heavy, too. I took a deep breath, turned the knob, and walked in. The secretary was on the phone, but she saw me and held up her pointer finger. I took that to mean I should wait one minute.

"Rehospitalization after T and A." She scribbled on a pink pad. "I'll let Jimmy's teacher know he'll be out for the rest of the week. Thanks for calling."

She hung up the phone. "What can I do for you, young man?"

"I lost a book that belongs to my mother."

"What's the name of the book?"

"It's by C. S. Lewis," I said. "The first book in a series he wrote for kids called the Chronicles of Narnia."

"The Chronicles of Narnia by C. S. Lewis." She wrote on the pad.

"That's the series, but the book is *The Lion, the Witch and the Wardrobe*."

"Okay." She scratched out part of what she'd written and scribbled again. Then she looked at me. "When did you last see it?"

"Before Christmas break."

"And where did you last see it?"

In Mr. Harding's hand.

I said quietly, "I think Mr. Harding might have it in his office."

"Oh, I see." She crossed her arms. "And did Mr. Harding happen to take it away from you?"

"Not exactly."

"What then? Exactly."

"Mrs. Carter actually gave it to him."

"And did Mrs. Carter actually take it from you?"

I looked at the snow melting off my boots onto the carpet. "I guess so."

"And why was that, do you think?"

I glanced back up. "Maybe because I was reading it during class."

The secretary covered her mouth for a second. "Tell you what—it's Matthew, isn't it?"

"Yes, Matthew Vos. That book is really old. It belonged to my mom before she got married."

"Before she got married?" She rubbed her mouth again. "Well, in that case, it's probably an antique."

"Yeah." I nodded slowly. "Maybe it's very valuable."

"Could be." She put her headphones into her ears and smiled. "I'll see what I can do."

"Okay." I backed toward the door. "Thanks."

She nodded and began typing.

I hung my backpack and coat in my locker, and slipped out of my boots. I pawed inside my backpack, but couldn't feel my shoes. I jerked the backpack open. No shoes. I put my boots back on. They were almost dry, but not too many other kids my age wore snow boots. I'd been eager to get rid of them. Now I was stuck with them for the whole day.

I wondered if the school could call Mom to bring my shoes. But I'd already bothered the secretary enough, and Mom was probably in the shower. She might even be back in bed if she were feeling sick again. I sighed, fished out my math book and notebook, and headed for class.

"Hey, PK-2." Josh met me coming down the hall. "Why do you still have your boots on? Planning to do some kicking?"

I'd like to do some kicking all right.

In math class, I couldn't remember a thing I'd learned about algebraic equations before Christmas break. In science, I was the only one who put up a hand when Mr. Bates asked if there were any creationists in class.

"I'm not going to say what God did or didn't do," he said. "But don't you think, Matthew, that he could have taken billions of years to create the world?"

My voice squeaked like a tiny mouse. "The Bible says he created it in six days."

"The Bible also says that a thousand years are like a day to God, doesn't it?"

"Yes." I scrunched lower in my seat.

When Josh and Dan saw me in the hall during break, they belted out "Bootman" to the tune of the Batman theme song.

In social studies, Mrs. Carter had the students take turns reading out of the textbook. Another of the most boring classes ever. I was tempted to read my new book, but I didn't want it sucked into the Black Hole.

At least Mom's book would keep it company.

Then came the worst. PE with Mr. Griswold. And I didn't have athletic shoes.

Rumor was that Mr. Griswold had been a Marine who'd invaded Grenada during Operation Urgent Fury.

He had a buzz cut and bulging biceps. And he insisted on appropriate footwear. One time when Alicia wore flat canvas shoes, he'd pulled her in front of the class and said this was an example of the kind of shoes we should not wear to gym class. Alicia's long red hair hung in front of her even redder face.

That shoe incident was fresh in my mind as I walked on weak legs down to the gym. Mr. Griswold blew his whistle and told us to form a line.

I walked over to him on jelly legs. "Ah, Mr. Griswold?"

"Vos, isn't it?" His voice boomed as loud as a cannon.

"Yes, sir." I gulped. "I forgot my shoes today."

He scowled down at me. "Now, Vos. You know the importance of appropriate footwear for physical activity, don't you?"

"I do, sir. I thought my gym shoes were in my backpack, but—when I got to school—they weren't."

I hadn't thought it was possible, but he scowled even harder. "You'll have to run in your socks, Vos. Leave your boots by the steps."

I set my boots beside the steps and slid on the slick floor into line with the other kids.

Mr. Griswold blew his whistle in three short bursts. "We'll begin today with a few laps. Williamson, you're the leader."

We ran around the gym, following Jason Williamson. I slipped and slid around every corner and had been passed by four other kids when the intercom crackled.

Mr. Griswold whistled and we all stopped. I slid into the backside of Heidi Fox or "Foxy" as she's called. The class roared with laughter.

Mr. Griswold whistled again and held up his hand for silence. "Yes?" he called. "What is it?"

"Is Matthew Vos there?" The intercom echoed in my head and through the gym.

"Yes."

"Please send him to the office."

My face had been flaming hot from bumping into Heidi, but at those words I felt every drop of blood drain from it. A cold sweat broke out on my forehead.

No one laughed now. The gym was as quiet as a tomb. As I walked past my classmates, they looked at me like I was a condemned man. I felt every stare as I put my freezing feet into my bulky boots. I thumped up the steps like a man ascending the gallows.

18

RESCUE AND REVELATION

I stood paralyzed outside the school office door.

And I thought it was scary going in earlier.

My stomach felt like a volcano about to erupt. And the lava was already in my throat. Taking a deep breath, I prayed. *Lord, help me.*

I gulped, raised my hand, and turned the knob.

The secretary still typed away with those tiny earphones in her ears. She looked up and smiled. "Go on into Mr. Harding's office."

I stumbled through the doorway on robot-stiff legs.

Mr. Harding smiled. He held Mom's book in his hands. The shoes I'd left at home sat on the floor in front of his desk. A man in a chair turned. It was Dad!

I don't know why, but tears sprang to my eyes. I ran to Dad and threw my arms around him, crying like a baby on his shoulder. He hugged me and patted my back. "It's okay, Matt."

"I've just had such a bad morning." I looked at him and tried to blink away my tears. "I forgot my shoes, and I couldn't remember anything in algebra class, and I was the only creationist in science, and I had to run in my socks during PE, and I slid right into Foxy's backside."

My dad raised his eyebrows, but kept patting my shoulder. "It'll be okay, Matt."

Mr. Harding cleared his throat. I'd forgotten him.

I wiped my cheeks with my sweater sleeve, but Dad fished a handkerchief from his shirt pocket and handed it to me. He always carried cloth ones that Mom washed and ironed because she says you never know when a pastor may need to offer a handkerchief.

I dabbed my eyes. My tears made the crisp white cloth turn dark and limp. I handed Dad the soggy hanky.

"It seems," Mr. Harding said, "that Matthew has had a rather trying morning."

Dad nodded. "I should say so."

"Matthew, your father and I have already discussed the little matter of your reading in class." He handed me Mom's book. "He assures me that it won't happen again."

I clutched the book against my chest. "It won't."

"Good." Mr. Harding pressed his fingertips together. "I'm very pleased to hear that."

"And," Dad said, "Mr. Harding is familiar with C. S. Lewis and his Chronicles of Narnia. He didn't realize the book was part of that series because he didn't take time to look at it when Mrs. Carter gave it to him."

Dad lifted my chin and looked into my eyes. "But regardless of what kind of book you were reading, you need to pay attention in class, right?"

"Right." Maybe I spoke louder than necessary.

"Mr. Harding," Dad gave him a friendly smile. "I wonder—could Matthew be excused from school for the rest of the day?"

"Well, certainly, Mr.—I mean—Reverend Vos," Mr. Harding stammered. "If that's what you want. You are his parent, after all."

"That's right." Dad also spoke a little too loudly. "And I think Matt needs to spend some time with me today."

My jaw dropped so far it almost hit my shirt.

"Ah, fine." Mr. Harding smiled with only his mouth. "I'll just—um—I'll just tell Ms. McBride to mark Matthew as an excused absence for the rest of the day."

Dad rubbed his hands together. "Excellent."

Before I knew it, I was sitting beside my dad in his car—Mom's book in one hand and my shoes in the other.

The snow still fell in big flakes. Dad turned on the wipers and I watched them go back and forth in their lazy way. "I'm sorry I cried."

"I'm not." Dad squeezed my shoulder. "If you hadn't, I wouldn't have known how much all these things were bothering you." He backed up the car. "Now we can spend time together and talk things over—man to man."

"Man to boy, you mean."

"Being a man isn't merely size or age, Matt." Dad peered both ways through the foggy windshield before he pulled out of the parking lot. "It's a matter of character. And you've got a great start on building godly character."

"I do?"

"You do. You love the Lord and you're trying to live for him every day. That's absolutely the most important part of becoming a man."

I don't always try to live for Jesus.

Dad cranked up the defroster. "Mom and I have both noticed that you're making an effort to get along better with John. Take yesterday morning—you almost said something negative about him, but you stopped yourself. That's a step in the right direction."

The wipers squeaked across the windshield.

Finally I noticed that Dad wasn't driving toward our house. He was heading the other direction. "Aren't we going home?"

"Nope. I'm taking you out to lunch. Mom isn't feeling well today and she's resting now, so we'll leave her alone a little longer."

Mom's sick again!

"What in the world is the matter with her, Dad? She overslept this morning. How come she feels so sick all the time?"

"Well—" Dad seemed to consider something serious.

He's figuring out how to tell me really bad news.

"I think you're old enough to handle this."

I knew it. Mom has cancer.

"The truth is—" He took a deep breath. "We think she's pregnant."

I stared at him. "Pregnant? Mom? You mean she's going to have a baby?"

"Yes, all symptoms indicate that."

"Then she doesn't have cancer?"

"No." Dad glanced at me with wide eyes. "She doesn't have cancer. Whatever gave you that idea?"

"Aunt Pam had cancer. She felt sick and slept a lot."

"That was different." His words tumbled out. "A different kind of sickness and a different kind of tired. I can assure you Mom does not have cancer."

"But it runs in families."

"That may be true, but Aunt Pam was married to my brother. She wasn't related to you except by marriage."

I should have realized that. But then I remembered something. "Mom's teaching Sunday school for Mrs. Larson because *she's* going to have a baby."

Dad chuckled. "Ironic, isn't it?"

"Yeah." Last semester's vocabulary word took on a whole new meaning. "It is ironic. Does John know this?"

"Nobody knows other than Mom and me. I wouldn't have told you yet except that I didn't want you to worry about her on top of everything else." He turned a corner. "Since no one else knows, I think you should keep it to yourself for a while. At least until we tell your brothers."

I'd never known anything John didn't already know. "I'll keep it a secret." I smiled. "Even from John."

"Good man." Dad squeezed my shoulder again. "I knew I could count on you." He braked for a stop sign. "Now, I have a few pressing questions." He looked both ways before pulling forward. "First, where would you like to go for lunch?"

"Pizza Ranch?"

"They don't offer the buffet during the day. We'd have to order."

"I don't mind if it takes longer, but don't you have work to do?"

"It's Monday—my day off. I can take the time."

"Great." I relaxed and smiled. Dad had never taken only me out to eat. "What are your other questions?"

"Well." Dad signaled for a turn. "I guess my next would be: Who in the world is Foxy?"

"Heidi Fox. Everybody calls her 'Foxy' because of her last name."

"Everybody?" He looked at me from the corners of his eyes. "Or just the guys?"

"Everybody, Dad. She's been 'Foxy' since the second grade."

"You mean everyone has called her by that nickname since then?"

"Sure." *What else could I mean?*

PIZZA FOR TWO

Dad ordered a large Stampede pizza. He said we'd bring home the leftovers for his lunch the next day to give Mom another break. Then he did something that hardly ever happened when we went out to eat. He sprung for soda. He even let me pick Dr. Pepper, which Mom never did because she claimed it was too high in caffeine—right up there with Mountain Dew.

We found a booth by the window. I tore the tip off my straw's wrapper and blew the paper tube at Dad. He blew his back at me. I grinned and stuck my straw in my plastic glass full of dark pop, ice cubes, and fizzy bubbles.

Through the window, I saw snow mounting up. "Do you think school will let out early?" I'd hate for that to happen when I'd already been rescued.

"Nope. It's melting when it hits the streets, so the buses should have no problem getting the kids home."

"I'm glad." I didn't say exactly why I was glad. I could keep more than one kind of secret. "Why is snow piling up on the sidewalks, but not on the streets?"

"Because the streets have been treated with salt." Dad rolled up our straw papers and placed them near the table's edge. "It'll have to get colder before the snow starts to stick. But the temperature's supposed to drop, so the streets may need to be plowed tonight."

"What's the plan for this afternoon?"

"I don't have a plan. It's my day off."

"What do you usually do on Mondays, Dad?"

"Well, generally, I don't schedule sermon writing or class preparation or visits." Dad grinned. "Then I see how many visits and other work I end up doing anyway."

"Not much of a day off."

"Not always. But after I bring John to practice, I go to the pastors' weekly prayer breakfast. Sometimes I hang out at the library."

"What about today?"

"I went home after breakfast to check on your mom. That's when I noticed your school shoes were still on the mat beside the back door. Luke's, too."

"Luke!"

"What?" Dad jerked his head. "What about him?"

"He'll be worried when I don't get on the bus."

"I'll call school and leave a message for his teacher. She can tell him you went home early."

"Great."

The waitress brought a couple of plates and our pizza. It looked huge, but I was starving.

After we'd stuffed ourselves for a while, Dad wiped his mouth with a napkin. "I still have a few questions."

"Shoot."

"About the book—"

"Oh, yeah. It's Mom's. I got it off the bookshelf in your office. I know I should've asked, but you were gone and Mom was busy and Adam had been telling me how great these Narnia books were, and I figured if Adam's parents let him read them, they had to be okay for kids, so I didn't think it would hurt if I just—sort of—borrowed it."

"I don't mind that you borrowed it, but I'd have preferred if you'd asked either Mom or me first."

"I know." I nodded. "I should have."

"And I definitely mind that you were reading it during class. You want to tell me why?"

"Mrs. Carter always makes the kids read aloud from the textbook." I looked at his eyes. "Dad, some of those kids are *real* slow readers. It's so boring to sit there and listen to them stumble through each paragraph. I can read a whole page about ten times before the class gets through it. I practically know the entire book by heart."

"I can understand that might be boring, but you need to pay attention in class."

"I know. Today I didn't get out *The Visual Dictionary of Special Military Forces* even though I really wanted to. I just sat there and read every paragraph, every sentence, over and over." I rolled my eyes.

"It doesn't sound like the most effective teaching method, but I'm glad you didn't give in to temptation. Maybe all that oral review will help you out on quizzes."

"Maybe." I wasn't so sure.

"I happen to know, however, that Mom's dad gave her that set of Narnia books and she probably wouldn't want any of them being bounced around in your backpack."

I suppose, deep down, I'd known she'd feel that way.

"I think—" Dad gave me another piece of pizza. "Since the book is fine and is going right back on the shelf where it belongs, and since Mom has so many other things on her mind right now—there's probably no need to tell her about something that's past and all settled."

I slowly chewed a big bite of pizza. Apparently I wasn't the only one who could keep a secret.

"We'll go home after lunch." Dad helped himself to more pizza. "I'll return the book to the shelf in the study. I'll call school so Luke knows you won't be riding the bus. And I'll run upstairs and tell Mom that you and I are spending some quality time together."

My mouth was full, so I only nodded.

"Now what were you saying about being the only creationist?"

After I swallowed, I told Dad the whole story. He listened without interrupting.

Then he asked about gym class, and I described Mr. Griswold and his shoe policy. He wanted to know about my classmates, so I told him about Dan's four-wheeler, Mike's BB gun, Josh's Ping-Pong table, and how they sometimes call me "PK."

"PK?" He looked surprised. "For Preacher's Kid? I thought that died in the seventies. That's what the neighborhood kids used to call me."

I knew Grandpa Vos was a minister, but I'd never thought about Dad being a PK. "I don't like being called 'PK.'" I glanced up. "But I'm proud to be your kid."

He squeezed my arm. "And I'm proud to be your dad."

We'd lost interest in the pizza, but it was almost gone anyway. The waitress brought a take-out box, and Dad put the leftovers in it. "What would you like to do after we stop at the house?"

"Is there enough snow for sledding? I'd like to try out my new Flexible Flyer."

Dad squinted out the window. "Not yet. And it's probably not cold enough for good sledding. But if this keeps up and the temperature drops, we could reassess the situation later. Say around 2:00 or 2:30."

"That would be awesome."

"What shall we do in the meantime?"

I twisted my napkin. "This probably sounds stupid—"

"Go ahead."

"Well, I've never gone with you on any visits or anything, and I'd sort of like to do that." Then I quickly added, "But I know it's your day off."

"I don't mind a few visits on my day off. Like I said, they often come up anyway. I actually should stop by the hospital and visit Jimmy Flanders."

"Jimmy's back in the hospital? Didn't he go home?"

"He did, but he was readmitted yesterday due to some unexpected bleeding."

I remembered the secretary talking on the phone. "Did he have a T and A?"

"Yep."

"What is that, anyway?"

"Tonsillectomy and Adenoidectomy, removal of the tonsils and adenoids. He'll probably be released soon, but I doubt he'll be back in school this week. It's great you're coming along—he'll be glad to see someone close to his age. If we're at the hospital, we should visit Mr. Vincent, too. He's not doing well at all."

"Is he the guy who didn't know if he'd go to heaven?"

"Well, yes, but I shouldn't tell you what people say when I visit them." Dad's face got a little red and he tugged at his collar. "After we stop at the hospital, we could visit Mrs. Miller and Mr. Houser. They both love company and neither one naps in the afternoon like most of the older folks in our congregation."

As if I didn't see enough of Mrs. Miller with piano lessons. "But by the time we finish all that, will we still have time for sledding?"

Dad leaned forward and looked in my eyes. "I know this great hill—" He stood and pulled on his coat. "We'd better get going. We've got places to go, people to see, hills to conquer."

SURPRISE, SURPRISE

Our first stop was home. Dad told me to stay in the car while he ran inside.

The car's windows gradually fogged up. Out of the corner of my eye, a huge shape appeared. I jerked my head around. A bear!

In a panic, I rubbed my window. It was Brutus, followed by Jenny's mom, who was wearing a hooded black coat with a bulky black scarf wrapped around her neck. She held onto the leash with both gloved hands close to Brutus's big head.

A squirrel ran across our front yard and scampered up a tree. Brutus leaped at it. Jenny's mom pulled on the leash. "No! Bad dog!" Brutus quit tugging and walked calmly beside her. Looked like Jenny could take some Brutus-walking lessons from her.

They walked on and turned left at the corner.

The wipers softly squeaked. The heater fan hummed. Dad sure was taking a long time.

I dug in my backpack for *The Visual Dictionary of Special Military Forces.* In the section about "Covert amphibious forces," I read how they disable enemy ships by attaching limpet mines to the hulls. A picture showed glass beads containing bright colors of acetone. Different colors indicated different hours of delay in the fuse, with red being the shortest time.

The heater hummed. The wipers swooshed back and forth, back and forth, like waves surging on the ocean.

I dropped backward from the ship's deck into the sea. Bubbles from my scuba tank swirled around me. I swam under water until a dark shape loomed ahead. The enemy ship. I swam closer and closer, until I was within arm's reach. Carefully I attached a limpet mine to the steel hull and screwed a red acetone bead into the delay fuse. Then I twisted to swim away quickly before—BAM!

I jumped at the thump. The back of the car bounced. Relief washed over me. The "explosion" that had woken me had been Dad slamming the trunk shut.

He opened the door and slid behind the wheel. "Mission accomplished." He fastened his seat buckle. "Pizza in the fridge, check. Book back on shelf, check. School called, check. Mom reassured, check. Sled in trunk, check."

I pointed to Dad's dress shoes. "Are you going to wear those for sledding?"

"Ah! Good point."

"I'll need my snow pants, too."

"Be right back."

When Dad came out of the house, he could barely squeeze through the back door because his arms were so full of winter gear. He dumped it all in the back seat.

He didn't drive in the direction of the hospital, but toward the business district.

I asked, "Does Mr. Houser live uptown?"

"Nope."

We couldn't be headed to Mrs. Miller's because she lived the other way. "Then where are we going?"

"Before we do any visits," Dad said, "we have to make one important stop."

He parked on the square downtown, right in front of the Dutch bakery. When I opened the car door, I inhaled a delicious aroma that smelled like warm donuts.

Dad paused on the sidewalk and took a deep breath. "Maybe we'll have to make two stops."

I wondered what he was up to. We walked down the block until he opened a store door.

The bookstore. Yes!

The inside smelled like new books. Music played with some guy singing about old acquaintances being forgot. A Valentine's display advertised, "Books for Lovers." The sign on a table of thick books in leather covers said, "Curl up with a Classic."

A tall lady with red streaks in long black hair came up to us. "May I help you?"

"Yes." Dad stuffed his gloves into his pockets. "We're looking for The Chronicles of Narnia by C. S. Lewis."

"Oh!" The lady clasped her hands together like Olive Oyl in a Popeye cartoon on one of Luke's videos. "A perennial favorite of children—and their parents." She seemed pretty excited, but I felt like shouting.

She led us to the children's section. "Here they are." She pointed to two different places. "We have hardback or mass market individual volumes. Or—" She picked up a box covered with shrink-wrap. "We have this nice set of softcovers in its own cardboard case."

She handed the box to me. The front side showed a unicorn with a bloody horn and the back showed an old man and a boy at the top of a tall castle tower.

The lady pointed to the back of the box, which listed the books. "The publisher put the books in chronological order, but I recommend reading them in publication order." She tapped her long, red fingernail on the listing. "Instead of reading *The Magician's Nephew* first, save it for next to last, right before *The Last Battle*."

"I second that." Dad reached out. "We'll take this set."

An idea came to me. "Do you have the Space Trilogy?"

"Oh, a discerning reader." The lady did her Olive Oyl imitation again before leading us around the bookshelf. "We have some copies in a very affordable mass market edition." She grabbed two books and ran her red-tipped nail along the shelf's edge. "Let's see—do we have the third one?" The nail stopped and tapped a book's spine triumphantly. "Here it is—only one left." She stacked the three books together and handed the pile to Dad, who looked at me with raised eyebrows.

The bell above the door tinkled, and a woman came into the store. She stomped her boots on the mat and shook snowflakes from her long scarf.

The lady waved her red-tipped fingers. "I'll leave you two to discuss it." She strolled over to greet the customer who'd just entered.

"What are you thinking?" Dad wrinkled his forehead. "Do you want both sets of books?"

"No." I shook my head. "I feel sort of guilty getting new books when John isn't getting anything—"

"What a great brother you are."

I felt even guiltier and turned to read titles on the bookshelf. I sucked in my breath in surprise. They had the Accidental Detectives series by Sigmund Brouwer! Did I dare ask Dad to spend more money?

"I'm sure John will enjoy these." Dad straightened the books in his hands. "I know I did when I was his age."

"So the ones in the study belong to you?"

"Yes. I bought them with my own money when I got my first after-school job." He headed toward the counter.

"That set probably means a lot to you then?"

"It has some sentimental value." Dad got in line behind a woman with a tall stack of books. He spoke over his shoulder. "I wouldn't mind if you guys read that set, but I think it's good for you to have your own copies of this kind of classic literature."

I stepped beside him and whispered. "But this will be a lot of money—"

Dad bent close. "While I was in the house, I talked to Mom about buying the Narnia books with your portion of the Christmas money Grandpa and Grandma Weaver sent, but we didn't discuss John." Dad held up the Trilogy books. "I'll buy these with his share."

"Good idea." I nodded. "But what about Luke?"

"We'll let Mom shop for him later. She might already have something in mind."

The clerk told the woman, "That will be $54.32."

"Oh, dear." She fumbled in a bulky purse. "My gift card is only for $50."

While she and the clerk discussed which book to take off the total, I tapped Dad's arm. "I don't suppose there'd be enough of my share to buy another book?"

"Maybe. What'd you have in mind?"

"A book by Sigmund Brouwer." I led him to the shelf. "These Accidental Detectives books are really good. And they're almost always checked out at the library."

I pulled *Lost Beneath Manhattan* from the shelf and held it up so Dad could look at it.

He scanned the cover. "Looks exciting."

"It is."

"How much?"

I flipped it over and pointed to the price.

Dad lowered the stack of books. "Put it on the pile."

"Thanks, Dad."

On our way back to the car, we stopped at the bakery. Dad bought three Dutch letters and a dozen cherry donut holes.

"Letters to share with Mrs. Miller and donut holes for Mr. Houser." Dad handed me the two packages. "But first we'll make our hospital calls."

21
AT THE HOSPITAL

In Mr. Vincent's hospital room, the lights were off and the blinds were closed. A yukky smell made my stomach queasy. Dad went in, but I hung back in the doorway.

A woman sat beside the bed with her head down. Dad touched her shoulder. "Hello, Mrs. James. How's your father today?"

She lifted her head and slowly shook it. "Fading fast."

Dad picked up the man's hand. "Mr. Vincent? Can you hear me? It's Pastor Vos."

The man's eyes flickered open. His mouth worked, but nothing came out. Finally, Mr.Vincent said, "Jesus." He smiled. "P-peace—in my heart."

Dad put both hands over Mr. Vincent's and prayed. When I opened my eyes, Dad gently laid down the old man's hand. In the light from the hall, it looked like wax. As white as the sheet except for bulging blue veins.

Mr. Vincent's eyes were still closed. I think he was sleeping. Dad shook hands with Mrs. James. "Call if you need me. Anytime. Day or night."

After we'd walked down another hall, I touched Dad's arm. "Is Mr. Vincent going to be okay?"

"Sure is." Dad smiled a little. "His mind is finally at rest. And his soul soon will be resting with Jesus in heaven." Then he pointed. "Here's Jimmy's room."

The room was bright. Music blared, "Transformers—more than meets the eye." Jimmy was propped on pillows, watching a TV that hung from the ceiling.

His cheeks and neck were puffy and the skin under his eyes was dark. He looked like a chipmunk with two black eyes. A tube was taped to the back of one hand. His mom sat beside the bed, knitting. When she saw us, she picked up the remote and muted the TV.

Dad shook her hand. "How are things going today?"

"Better than yesterday." Mrs. Flanders stuffed her knitting into a big bag. "They're taking out his IV this afternoon, and—if he keeps liquids down—he may go home tomorrow."

"Great."

Jimmy still stared at the silent TV. His mom pushed a button on the remote and shut it off. "We can finish watching that after Pastor Tim and Matthew leave."

He scowled. "Okay."

His mom smiled at Dad and shrugged. "Sorry. He's had a rough couple of days."

"I understand." Dad put a hand on the bed railing. "We won't take much time, Jimmy. I just wanted to see how you were doing. I'm glad you're feeling a bit better."

Jimmy looked at me. "Did school let out early?"

"It did for Matt." Dad put his arm over my shoulders. "We're having some father-son quality time."

Mrs. Flanders smiled. "We appreciate you spending part of it visiting us."

Dad took his thin Bible from his shirt pocket. "You've had some scary experiences, Jimmy." He flipped pages.

"And I thought you might like to hear what God says in Psalm 56."

One of the things Dad read was, "When I am afraid, I put my trust in you." He talked about how we can trust God to take care of us even when frightening things happen. Then he held Jimmy's hand—the one without the IV—and prayed.

After prayer, Jimmy's mom stood and straightened his blanket. "Thanks so much, Pastor Tim. That was just what the doctor ordered."

"I'm glad it was helpful." Dad shook her hand again. "Let me know how things go."

"I will."

As we walked through the slushy parking lot back to our car, Dad put his hand on my shoulder. "What'd you think of your first hospital visits, Matt?"

I shook my head. "I didn't care for them much. Do you like doing that, Dad?"

Dad unlocked the car. "Not seeing people suffer, but I love bringing God's hope and comfort when they do."

I got in and buckled my seat belt. Dad's job was harder than I thought.

WHITE AS SNOW

At Mrs. Miller's, we parked beside the alley and walked to the back door. When she opened it, she smiled wide. "What a nice surprise. Father and son. Come in, come in."

Dad led the way into her kitchen as if he'd been there lots of times. "I hope you don't mind us dropping in unannounced."

"Not at all. You know I'm always happy to see you. And how special that you brought Matthew with you this time. Did school dismiss early?"

"Matt and I are having a little father and son time."

"Isn't that nice? Have a seat." She pulled out a narrow kitchen chair and smiled over its tall back. "Matthew, do you like hot cocoa?"

"Sure." Who didn't?

Mrs. Miller's kitchen smelled wonderful. Homemade bread cooled on a rack on the yellow tablecloth. A brilliant parakeet twittered in a cage beside the window.

Mrs. Miller put water in a pan and turned on the burner. Blue flames shot up around the pan and she quickly turned it lower. She measured cocoa and sugar into a cup, and then poured milk into another one. "Excuse me a minute." She went into the living room.

The bird chirped and the blue flame hissed. Mrs. Miller came back with white china cups and saucers decorated with red roses and green leaves.

She stirred the cocoa and sugar into the boiling water and smiled at me. "You have to boil this for one minute." After a while, she added milk and turned down the heat. "You can't let it boil after you add the milk." Pretty soon she shut off the flame and stirred in a little vanilla. Finally she poured the hot concoction into our cups.

When I made hot chocolate, I microwaved water in a mug and added instant mix.

"I'm afraid I don't have those cute little marsh-mallows." She sighed. "I just can't get through a whole bag before they turn hard, so I've given up buying them."

"That's okay." Dad handed her a bakery bag. "We brought some sugar."

She peeked inside. "Dutch letters. My favorite." She pulled out the S-shaped pastries and set one on a napkin in front of each of us. My mouth watered at the smell of the almond filling.

We ate pastries and drank chocolate as Mrs. Miller told us about the first time she flew in an airplane. "Of course, that was before I had my pilot's license."

I nearly spewed chocolate all over her clean table-cloth. "Pilot's license? You fly planes?"

"Oh, not since I got married. But I did when I was still single. I was a buyer for a big department store chain, and I'd ride the train to New York on my purchasing trips. One day I met another young woman on the train, and we really hit it off. She had her pilot's license, and that inspired me. So when I returned, I started lessons at the municipal airport."

Dad grinned. "Mrs. Miller's sort of like a Transformer, isn't she, Matt? There's more to her than meets the eye."

"I'll say."

Then Mrs. Miller told a suspenseful story about when the man teaching her suddenly passed out and she had to land the plane by herself—after only six hours of instruction. When she finished, I let out a long sigh of relief at the good ending and lifted my cup to my lips. My cocoa was cold.

Mrs. Miller lifted the pan. "Shall I warm that up for you, Matthew?"

I shook my head. "No, thanks, Mrs. Miller. That was the best hot chocolate I've ever had, but I can't drink any more." I patted my bulging tummy. "We had a big lunch. And I never had a whole Dutch letter to myself before."

She chuckled as she cleared off the table. Then she sat down, folded her hands, and looked at Dad.

He opened his Bible. "Today's weather reminds me of Isaiah 1. I'll read verses twelve through twenty."

Listening for something related to weather, I heard Dad read, ". . . though your sins are like scarlet, they shall be as white as snow."

When Dad finished, Mrs. Miller gazed out the window. "Whenever I see fresh snow cover up the dirty ground, I thank God for making my sins white as snow."

Dad prayed, and then we shook hands with her. She held mine with both of hers. "Thank you so much for coming with your father today, Matthew."

"It was fun," I answered truthfully.

She let go of my hand. "I've been thinking about what you said Saturday."

Oh, no! She's going to tell Dad that I was rude.

She smiled. "I'm scouting around for an exercise book without so many boring scales."

I bounced on my toes. "Thank you, thank you."

She laughed like a girl. "I'm also looking for an easy hymn book. We could take a new song with each lesson and call it our 'Hymn-of-the-Week' program. How does that sound?"

"Terrific."

She looked in my eyes. "If you practice your songs for a half hour every day this week, I'll start our 'Hymn-of-the-Week' program on Saturday. Is it a deal?"

"It's a deal." We shook on it.

Mrs. Miller covered the loaf of bread with Saran Wrap. "I know Lisa's a busy mother. I'm sure she'll appreciate some homemade bread."

Dad zipped his coat. "But you made that for yourself."

She waved a hand. "My son gave me a bread maker for Christmas. I'll just make another loaf." She grinned and whispered, as if sharing a secret. "It's really not much work anymore."

On the way over to Mr. Houser's, I thought about how different he was from Mrs. Miller. He used a cane and didn't come to church during the winter. And instead of having his own home, he lived in a building with lots of other old people.

When we knocked on his door, he yelled, "Come in. It's not locked."

He sat in a big chair, watching TV. When he saw us, his face split into a huge smile and he shut off the TV with a remote. "Well, hello, Dominee." His voice boomed louder than Mr. Griswold's. "And who's this with you? Dominee-in-training?"

Dad explained I'd wanted to go along on some visits.

"Like I said. Dominee-in-training." When he laughed, his big belly jiggled like Mom's molded Jell-O salad.

He motioned for us to sit, but when I walked past him, he grabbed my arm. "Yust a minute, young man." He leaned close. His breath smelled like black licorice. "You like pop?"

I'd already had more than a week's worth of my caffeine allowance, and my stomach was about to burst with hot chocolate and Dutch letter on top of Dr. Pepper and more pizza than I'd ever eaten. But the only honest answer to Mr. Houser's question was, "Yes."

"You'll find some cans of pop in the fridge. Get one for your papa, too."

There were several soda cans in the fridge, all Orange Crush. I knew for a fact Dad didn't like Orange Crush. He'd told me it was the only kind he'd been allowed to drink for free when he'd worked at a grocery store, so he'd drunk it every day. Since then, he just didn't care much for it. But I took two cans and brought one to Dad.

He opened his and took a big swig. I opened mine and took a small sip. Dad offered the donut holes to Mr. Houser. He smacked his lips. "Cherry. Goot. My very favorite."

Mr. Houser passed me the bag. I took a donut hole and handed the sack to Dad, who took one and gave the bag to Mr. Houser. He popped another into his mouth and passed the bag to me.

I looked into it and smelled the cherry aroma, but for the first time in my life I'd had the opportunity to test Mom's theory that too much sugar could make you sick. And I believed she just might be right.

I handed the bag to Dad without taking any donut holes. He held it for a bit, while he talked, and then he gave it to Mr. Houser, who took another donut hole and passed me the bag.

We kept up that "pass-the-bag" routine with only Mr. Houser helping himself, until he had eaten all the donut holes. He looked into the sack with surprise. "Ach! Sorry, young man." His eyes smiled, although his mouth frowned. "I guess I took the last one."

I held up a hand. "No problem. Really."

He crumpled the bag and handed it to me. "The garbage is under the sink."

I threw away the sack. Then I quietly poured my soda down the drain, while I looked around Mr. Houser's apartment. His whole place was smaller than our kitchen and den. It smelled like gym socks and fried fish.

Mr. Houser told Dad how much his muscles ached when the weather changed. "But, I'm not complaining. At least I'm not in a nursing home yet, right, Dominee?"

"That's right. And you're still a strong prayer warrior."

"You betcha. An old man like me can still pray for the kinderen, like this one, yah?" Mr. Houser grabbed my arm again as I walked past. "What a fine young man he's getting to be." He blasted my face with breath that now smelled like licorice and cherries.

He shook his head. "I'm yust sorry you cannot go to Christian school—like my boys."

He dropped my arm, but I didn't leave his side. "They went to Christian school? In this town?"

"Yah. It was a fine school."

"What happened to it?"

"It closed." His whole face frowned. "Too many families moved away. First the canning factory shut down. Then lots of farmers lost their shirts raising hogs. A few even lost their farms." He sighed. "Other churches stopped supporting the school, and it got to be too much for yust our congregation." He looked at Dad. "I was on the Board, you know."

"I didn't know." Dad gazed at Mr. Houser. "Was that when the decision was made to shut down the school?"

"No." Mr. Houser smacked the arm of his chair with his huge palm. "I would never have let them close that school. My father and uncle helped start it. The Board should have kept it going, but no one listened to me."

"I'd like to hear more about this." Dad took out his Bible. "But Matt and I have an important appointment this afternoon."

"Ach! I hope it's not with the dentist." Mr. Houser turned toward me and pulled a funny face.

I grinned. "No, it's not."

"Actually," Dad said, "it's with that sledding hill out on the Beyer farm."

"Ha!" Mr. Houser jabbed a beefy finger at Dad. "That is a goot one. The best in the county. You better hurry up and get out there, Dominee."

"Would you like me to read a Psalm?"

"Yah, that would be goot. How about Psalm 51?"

Dad found it. "I'll read through verse seventeen."

Because I was looking at the family pictures covering the walls, I wasn't paying attention until I heard Dad read, "Wash me, and I shall be whiter than snow."

After Dad finished, Mr. Houser said, "Yah, when I see God cover up the mud with clean snow, I think about how Christ covers my filthy sins with his righteousness."

Mr. Houser is more like Mrs. Miller than I thought.

When we walked to the car, it was much colder. Our footsteps crunched in the new snow. Dad pulled up his sleeve to check his watch. "It's 2:30 on the nose." He clapped his gloved hands. "Time to show you that hill."

KEEPING SECRETS

I cranked up the car heater. "That was fun. The colder it got, the faster the sled flew."

Dad turned onto the highway. "It would have been better if we'd had a ski lift."

"It sure took a lot longer to get up than down."

The sledding hill had been far out in the country. By the time we got back into town, the streetlights began to flicker on. As we drove into the driveway, our headlights shone on the garage door in two circles that got smaller and smaller as we pulled closer.

Inside, the table was set, and Mom stirred something that steamed in a big pot on the stove. Luke played with Hot Wheels on the den floor. John closed the book he'd been reading and held it under his crossed arms as he walked down the hall. I was pretty sure it was Dad's copy of *Out of the Silent Planet*, but I didn't say anything.

"Well, hello, finally." Mom grinned. "I was beginning to think I'd have to call the council president and tell him the pastor would be late for tonight's meeting."

Dad thumped his palm against his forehead. "I forgot all about that meeting."

"How could you forget?" Mom turned off the burner. "Isn't a new proposal being presented tonight?"

"Right, right." Dad pulled off his stocking cap. "Will I have time to shower?"

"Sure. Looks like you'll both need to do that after dinner. You two have fun?"

"It was awesome." I hung up my coat. "But walking back up that hill was a real killer."

"Yeah." Dad ran his hand through his damp hair. "We worked up a sweat."

"I see that." Mom laughed. "Hang your wet stuff in the basement, and then we'll eat."

I slipped off my drippy snow pants. "What're we having?"

"Chicken soup." Mom grabbed a potholder. "There should be plenty left over for times I don't feel well."

I glanced at Dad. Neither of us said anything about why Mom hadn't been feeling well.

One of Luke's Hot Wheels rolled under the table and he ran after it. When he saw Dad and me, he scowled. "How come I didn't get to go sledding with Daddy?"

"Luke Chadwick, how many times do I have to tell you?" Mom set the soup pan on the table. "This was Matt's special day with Dad. You can have one another time." She leaned over and touched his lips with one finger. "Remember what I told you? Not another word."

After dinner, Dad gave John the new Space Trilogy set. I decided to get piano practice out of the way while I waited for the shower. I was eager to break open my Narnia books as soon as possible.

As I searched for my assigned song in the last book, I heard Dad come into the kitchen and talk to Mom. "It will be interesting to see how this proposal is received."

"Let's hope it gets unanimous approval."

"It should, but I've been surprised before."

Mom's voice was soft. "I'll be praying."

"So will I." Dad's voice was muffled, maybe by a kiss. I was glad I was in another room.

"Matt," Mom called. "That wasn't a half hour yet."

Finally—after piano practice and a quick shower—I was alone in my room, looking at my new books. Accidental Detectives or Narnia? It was a tough choice. I'd already started the first Narnia book, and Adam was always asking about it. I'd better finish it first. I sighed and put the Sigmund Brouwer book down. Then I carefully slit open the plastic wrap on my Narnia set. I examined each book's cover before sliding it back into the box in the order I wanted to read it. Once I'd finished *The Lion, the Witch and the Wardrobe*. And after *Lost Beneath Manhattan*.

Luke came in and lifted the lid on his bin of Legos. He pawed through them, making a terrible racket. I decided to find my favorite reading spot in the den.

In the hall, I noticed John's door was open. *Lord, please make John a nicer brother.*

He lay on his bed, reading. I knocked on the door frame. "Hey."

He lifted his head. "Hey, yourself, what's up?"

"Not much." I walked in. "Watcha reading?"

"*Perelanda*, the second book in the Space Trilogy. Thanks for asking Dad to get the set for me, by the way."

"You're welcome. You're not starting with the first book?"

He looked back down at the page. "I actually finished that one already."

"And it's back on the shelf in the study?"

"Yeah." John's head shot up. "How'd you know that?"

"Just a good guess. I thought that's where you were going with it when we came home." He just stared at me, so I changed the subject. "Did you know Dad used to be called PK?"

"No, really?"

"Really. He told me so today."

"I never knew that."

And that makes two things I learned today that you didn't know.

"Well, I want to read my new books, too." I gave a cool little wave. "See ya later, bro."

In the den, I stretched out on the couch and opened *The Lion, the Witch and the Wardrobe* to the chapter I'd been reading before the book disappeared in the Black Hole. I read about how all the children came into Narnia wearing fur coats, and how they met the beavers.

Mom came into the den and bent over, picking up Hot Wheels Luke had left on the floor.

I remembered something I wanted to ask. "Mom, what does 'Dominee' mean?"

Mom looked up with strands of hair falling over her face. "'Domini' is Latin for lord or master. Why on earth are you asking?"

"Because it's what old Mr. Loursma called Dad when he brought over the new water heater and what Mr. Houser called Dad when we visited him this afternoon."

"Oh, that's Dutch. It's another word for Reverend." She tucked back her hair. "And don't call Mr. Loursma, 'old' Mr. Loursma."

"I just mean that he's the old man."

"The *older* man."

"Right." I had more questions for her. "I didn't know you knew other languages."

"I don't, really." She dropped a handful of cars into the toy box. "I studied Latin in high school, so I can read it pretty well. But I can't write it or speak it. Your Aunt Lora can. She's the Latin expert in the family."

"You know Dutch, too."

"Only a few words I've picked up since we moved here. 'Dominee' happens to be one I know because some people call your dad that."

"Mr. Houser called me, 'Dominee-in-training.'"

"Did he?" She smiled and sat on the couch by my feet. She looked pretty with her hair swooped across her forehead above her warm eyes. "Well, Matt." She patted my knee. "Men who feel called to the ministry must be convinced it's God calling them. That they're not just responding to someone else's expectations, or pressure from family or friends—even church members."

Did Mr. Houser think I wanted to be a minister? I was only curious about visits. Time to change the subject. "How long since you've read the Chronicles of Narnia?"

"It's been quite a few years." Mom leaned back on the couch cushions. "But I've read them several times. Grandpa Weaver bought me a set when I was about your age. I loved them, so I was glad your dad came up with the idea of buying a set for you with Christmas money."

I really didn't want to talk about the set Grandpa had bought for her. It was time to change the subject again. "What's this new proposal the council is voting on tonight?"

"I suppose I shouldn't say much about it, but Dad will probably fill you in tomorrow anyway. And since it will significantly affect our family, I think you have a right to know."

I sat up straight. How could it "significantly affect" our family?

Mom tucked her feet beneath her. "Celebration Church is building a new facility, so the proposal is for our church to buy their old property."

"Celebration? Isn't that the church just a few blocks from here?"

"That's the one."

"That building is a lot bigger, isn't it?"

"Yes. Two educational wings, so we wouldn't have fifth grade meeting in our living room." She smiled widely. "And the parsonage is bigger, too."

"How many bedrooms?"

"I don't know for sure, but I'm guessing there are more than three."

"Maybe I could have my own room."

She grinned. "I think that's a distinct possibility."

And that's one more thing I know that John doesn't.

ANTICIPATION

CRASH!

I bolted upright in bed. Light flashed back and forth across the bedroom floor. Outside a motor rumbled. Someone shouted. I ran to the window.

The big blade of a snowplow pressed against the streetlight. The pole leaned at an angle, swaying. A shape ran down the sidewalk—Brutus!

I dashed downstairs. Dad was pulling on his coat.

"What happened?"

"A snowplow had an accident." He zipped up. "I'm going out to check."

"Can I come, too?"

Dad paused with his hand on the doorknob. "Slip your snow pants over your pajamas. Wear your warm coat and put on a cap and gloves. It's very cold this morning."

I bundled up and was outside in no time. I ran toward a crowd of people at the corner.

"Stay back from the streetlamp," Dad called. "It might fall."

A police car with flashing lights drove up and parked crossways in the street.

I dashed over to Dad. "How did it happen?"

"Something ran in front of the plow, and the driver veered to miss it."

"It was Brutus."

Dad turned toward me. "You think so?"

"I saw him running away right after the crash."

"You did? How did you see that?"

"From my bedroom window."

Dad glanced up at my window and then back at the snowplow. The excited driver talked to the policeman. "It was huge!" He threw his arms in the air. "It looked like a bear!"

"Come with me." Dad jerked his head. "We ought to talk to that officer."

He led me through the crowd and then stepped forward. "Excuse me, sir." He gestured toward me. "My son has some information that might prove helpful."

"Yes?" The police officer looked down at me. "What is it, son?"

"I ran to the window as soon as I heard the crash and saw the neighbor's dog running down the sidewalk."

"This your house? Which window?"

"That one right there." I pointed up to my window beneath the peak.

"I see." The officer wrote in his notebook. "What direction did the dog go?"

"That way." I pointed down the sidewalk. The falling snow was rapidly filling gigantic Brutus prints.

"Anyone with the dog?"

"No, sir."

The snowplow driver shook his head. "But it was way bigger than a dog, Sergeant."

Dad said, "Brutus is a Bull Mastiff–St. Bernard mix. He's very big."

I nodded. "About as big as a bear."

"All right." The policeman made another note. "And who owns this monster dog?"

"The Bergmans." Dad pointed to their house. "They live right there."

The officer nodded and jotted something down. He closed his notebook and slipped it in his pocket. Then he looked at the crowd. "Okay, people." He waved his hand. "The excitement's over. You can all go home and get back to your regular business."

He turned to the snowplow driver. "You'll have to come down to the station and make a report. I'll talk to the dog's owner." He headed toward his car. "But first I'm going to call for a city crew to take care of that light."

"C'mon, Matt." Dad nudged my arm. "We'd better get back inside."

When we came in, Mom and Luke sat at the table. John peered out the kitchen window. He turned. "What happened?"

Dad told them all about it while we took off our coats and boots.

Mom frowned. "It's too bad for the Bergmans. I hope they don't get into trouble."

Dad poured himself some coffee. "And I feel sorry for the poor truck driver." He wrapped his hands around the steaming cup. "I hope he doesn't lose his job for having an accident. At least no one was hurt. It could have been a lot worse."

"Look at the time." Mom pointed to the clock. "You boys need to get ready for school."

My bare feet were freezing on the cold kitchen floor. "Will we have school today? Isn't there too much snow?"

"The streets are almost cleared." Dad sipped some coffee. "I listened to the radio earlier and there wasn't even one delay, let alone a cancellation. Hop to it." He put his hand on Mom's shoulder. "You stay sitting, Lisa." He kissed her cheek. "I'll make breakfast this morning."

At breakfast, John scarfed his oatmeal. Luke shaped his into a mountain. I tried to choke mine down. Mom wasn't eating much either. For once, I knew how she felt.

Dad tapped his spoon on the side of his bowl. "I have an Announcement." And he said it with a capital A.

"Last night the council unanimously passed the Building and Grounds Committee's new proposal, and the congregation will soon vote on it."

John helped himself to more oatmeal. "What *is* this proposal, Dad?"

"You've probably heard about the new facility that Celebration Church is building?"

"It's by the high school." John sprinkled about a cup of sugar over his oatmeal. No wonder he didn't mind the stuff. "Looks like Vets Auditorium in Des Moines."

"That's it." Dad nodded. "They hope to move into the new facility this summer."

"So?" John stuffed a gooey spoonful into his mouth.

"So." Dad's smile widened. "The proposal is for our church to purchase Celebration's old building, which is newer, bigger, and has more parking than our church. And the price is much lower than the cost of buying land and building a new church. It's a bargain."

I poked at the slimy glob in my bowl. "What would happen to our old church?"

"That's another great thing about this proposal." Dad rubbed his hands. "The Evangelical Free congregation is interested in purchasing our church and parsonage."

John grinned as he lifted his juice glass. "Sounds like musical chairs, only with church buildings."

"Is someone going to buy our house?" asked Luke. "Where would we live?"

"In a bigger house." Dad said. "The Celebration parsonage, right next to their current building, is included in this rock-bottom offer. Pastor Max and his family recently moved into a home of their own, so the parsonage is vacant."

Mom stirred her oatmeal. "What do you know about that house?"

"According to information presented last night, it's a large ranch style with a walk-out basement. The main floor includes kitchen, living room, study, laundry room, two bedrooms, and a full bath." Dad plopped an oatmeal blob into his bowl. "The basement has a recreation room, three bedrooms, and a bathroom with a shower."

I counted on my fingers. "Five bedrooms? I can have my own room even if—"

Dad tilted his head toward me and tightened his lips.

"—even if—if Luke has a room all to himself."

"Yes." Mom twirled a strand of her hair. "Five bedrooms would be wonderful right about now."

"I just don't see how anyone can object," Dad said. "It seems the ideal solution."

John snorted. "Someone always objects." His spoon scraped the bottom of his bowl. "I'll bet old man Dennison will complain at the congregational meeting.

From what I hear, he always makes a fuss about everything."

"He does usually address every issue." Dad frowned. "But if you must mention him, please call him 'Mr. Dennison' and drop the 'old.'"

"Okay." John wiped his mouth with his napkin. "I was in that basement once when Gabe invited me to a youth party. They had a Ping-Pong table down there."

I swiveled toward him. "Did you see the bedrooms?"

"Yeah. Gabe showed them to some of us guys." He scrunched up his eyes, like he was trying to remember. "They were all good-sized, but the one in the far corner was biggest." He widened his eyes and turned toward me. "If we move there, I've got dibs on that one."

I didn't care if he had the biggest bedroom. All I wanted was one to myself.

Even if Mom has a baby—like I almost blurted out—there will be enough for everyone, including one for me, myself, and I.

Mom shook her head. "Aren't we counting our chickens before they're hatched? We have to wait until the congregation votes."

"That's right." Dad nodded. "The information is being mailed out to church members today and the congregational meeting will be held very soon."

Mom sipped juice, looking thoughtful. "I wonder if the kitchen has more counter space."

Who cares about counter space? I just want a room—and a bed—of my own.

DROOL BLUES AND CAMPOREE NEWS

Stuck between sleeping and waking, I felt water drip on my face like a Chinese torture. I woke with Luke's head pressed against mine. Drool from his open mouth ran down my cheek.

"Ugh! Gross!" I pushed him away. "Get on your own side, Luke."

He only moaned and rolled over.

I sprinted down to the bathroom, grabbed a washcloth, and scrubbed every inch of my face. I even washed my tongue with the soapy cloth, but that made me gag.

"You're up early, Matt." Dad peeked through the doorway. "What's the problem?"

"That disgusting Luke was drooling all over my face. Who knows? Some might even have got in my mouth." I tossed the cloth in the sink and grabbed his sleeve. "Dad, can I *please* sleep on the den couch tonight?"

"I don't know." Dad rubbed his morning chin stubble. "I'll have to talk that one over with your mother."

"I don't have to sleep on the living room couch, I know it's newer. But the den couch is old. It's already stained. It won't hurt if I sleep on it."

"Calm down." Dad patted my head. "I said I'd talk to Mom about it. Why don't you get ready for school?"

"What day is it?"

"Wednesday."

Cadets tonight! We're sure to hear about Camporee.

At the bus stop, the guys splatted snowballs against the sign. The two little sisters giggled with each other. But Jenny stood alone.

I walked over to her. "Hi, Jenny. You been sick? You didn't ride the bus yesterday."

"I'm fine. What with one thing and another, we got late and Dad took me to school."

The Brutus incident.

"Did the policeman come to your house?"

"Yes." For the first time in my entire life, I saw Jenny without a smile.

"Are you guys in trouble?"

"The officer gave us a warning about keeping Brutus on a leash." Jenny looked at her boots. "Dad had let him out in the backyard, but he ran off. Chasing a squirrel." She looked up with firm lips. "We're going to put a fence around the back yard so he doesn't take off again."

"Sounds like a good plan."

I was glad her family hadn't gotten into too much trouble. And I was even happier that they'd keep Brutus penned up from now on.

On the bus, I sat beside Josh like usual. He bragged about playing Ping-Pong with his older brother, Eric. I tuned him out while I thought about Camporee.

During all my classes, I couldn't stop thinking about Camporee. Would it be in the mountains? Would I be old enough to go?

As soon as I got home from school, I rushed into the living room and sat at the piano.

Mom walked in while I was playing my first song. "Matt, I'm really proud of the way you're being so responsible about practice."

"If I do it for a half hour every day this week, Mrs. Miller's going to teach me a hymn."

"Really? Hymns are pretty hard to learn."

"She's getting an easy book for me."

"That's nice of her. You certainly have been doing your part. And it's been a big relief for me not to have to remind you every day."

"How soon can we eat dinner?" I shut that book and got out the next one. "Will there be time for Adam to come over before Cadets?"

"I think so, but what about your homework?"

"I hardly have any. I can do it before dinner."

"Okay. I'll call Susan and see if they can drop off Adam and Drew about 6:15. We should be finished eating by then. That will give you a little time together before you walk over to church. How does that sound?"

"Great." I pounded out my next song.

At dinner I slurped my chicken soup in record time. The clock read 5:54.

"Eat up, Luke." *He eats as slow as he walks.*

Dad refilled his bowl. "What's your hurry, Matt?"

Mom reached for a cracker. "Adam and Andrew are coming over after dinner."

I wiped my mouth, and then put my dirty napkin and spoon in my empty bowl. "Dad, did you talk to Mom yet about you know what?"

John glanced up. "What?"

Luke echoed. "What?"

Mom's forehead wrinkled. "Talk to me about what?"

Dad stirred his soup. "Matt sleeping on the couch in the den."

"Oh, that." Mom crumbled the cracker into her soup. "We discussed it at lunch, but I'm still considering it."

"Did Dad tell you that Luke drooled in my mouth?" I clenched my fists. "I could get sick from those kinds of germs, probably something really serious, like—like bubonic plague."

Dad cleared his throat. "You're not going to get the plague."

"I know sharing a bed with Luke can be annoying," Mom said. "But if you sleep in the den, it would be another set of sheets to wash each week. And I'd have to fold and put away your bedding every morning. That's a lot of extra work."

I held up my hand. "I solemnly promise to fold the sheets and blankets and put them away every day."

Mom frowned. "I don't know."

"It would only be temporary," I said. "If the proposal passes, we'll be moving to a bigger house and I'll have my own room."

"Let's hope so." She tilted her head. "I'll consider it."

"How long are you going to think about it, Mom?" I leaned forward. I really didn't want to spend another night with Luke, the drool ghoul.

"This evening. I'll let you know when you get home from Cadets."

After dinner, I ran upstairs to put on my gray Cadet shirt before Adam and Drew came. As I walked back down the steps, slipping up the leather slider that held my blue scarf around my neck, I heard my parents talking in the kitchen.

"I remember sleeping with my restless brother," Dad said. "It was not fun."

I stopped and held my breath.

Mom answered, "I know, but I just don't think I can handle any extra work right now."

"We could make it conditional. As long as he puts away the bedding every morning, he can sleep there. But if he forgets, he's back upstairs with Luke."

"Good idea. And he has been very responsible with his piano practices this week."

I silently pumped a fist in the air. My hard work was paying off.

Mom kept talking. "But we wouldn't be able to watch a movie or read in the den after the kids are in bed."

"That's true."

Oh, no!

The doorbell rang and I ran down. "I'll get it!"

Adam and Drew stood grinning on the front step.

"Hi, guys, come on in." After I closed the door behind them, I said, "Adam, I finished *The Lion, the Witch and the Wardrobe* last night."

"Finally. What did you think?"

"It was great."

Drew had read the book, too, so we talked about all the exciting parts while we played with my Legos on the coffee table in the den. Adam said how much Aslan reminded him of Jesus, and I said especially when he gave his life for Edmund. Then we each shared everything we'd ever heard about Camporee. Before we knew it, Mom told us it was time to walk over to Cadets.

I slipped on my coat. "I sure hope they announce something about Camporee."

Adam waved a hand. "Oh, they will. It's this summer. They've got to let us know."

Drew pulled his hood over his head and tied the strings. "I hope we're old enough to go."

I didn't think Drew would be. But he'd hate to miss going with Adam. Those two really enjoyed doing things together. A big difference from me and my brothers.

Mr. Flanders, our head counselor, led opening ceremonies. Then he passed out copies of the newest *Crusader* magazine. "The 1996 Cadet International Camporee will be held near Banff, Alberta, from July 24–31. Mark your calendars and talk to your parents about attending. You'll find the registration form and more information in this January issue."

The magazine cover showed a bighorn ram and snow-covered mountain peaks. Bold letters proclaimed KAMP KANANASKIS, ALBERTA across the top of an oval, and CADET INTERNATIONAL CAMPOREE across the bottom. The magazine's center was a two-page picture of mountains reflected in a lake. A full moon shone in a deep blue sky. The heading said, "Twilight comes to Kananaskis Country."

I flipped a page forward and found the list of requirements. I read: "Must be 12 years of age on or before December 31, 1996."

I'd be twelve in November. I could go!

I looked at Adam. His birthday was in June. He gave me a thumbs-up sign.

We both looked at Drew. He wouldn't turn twelve until next year. He stared at the floor.

"Now." Mr. Flanders clapped his hands. "You cadets who meet the age requirement must double-check that you've also met the badge requirements." He tapped a list in the magazine. "Very important." He held up some papers and raised his voice above the growing noise of excited murmurs. "You must complete these forms: parental/guardian permission form, health card, and club approval form. A registration fee is required for each camper."

Sudden silence. Every cadet held his breath.

"The total registration fee is $160."

The only sound was him shuffling papers. "But the Hawkeye Council will pay half the registration fee." He smiled. "Each Cadet needs to come up with only $80."

We exhaled. Everyone started talking and laughing.

Mr. Flanders blew his whistle. "Another $120 for transportation is due at registration." He cleared his throat. "We expect the total cost of transportation will be around $450."

Wow! $450! Can Mom and Dad afford that?

"That's a lot of money," someone said from the back.

Mr. Flanders nodded. "It's expensive because we'll fly from Des Moines to Calgary. But we're trying to help parents by making part of the expense due now and part of it due later."

He ticked off on his fingers. "Your completed registration form, the $80 toward the registration fee, and the $120 for transportation must be sent in before Thursday, February 15. That's $200 due by February 15. Be sure to discuss this with your parents."

After Cadets, Adam and I walked outside together. I took a deep breath. "Camporee is going to be a lot more expensive than I thought."

"I know." He put up one hand. "But at least we're old enough to go."

I returned his high five. "I'm sorry about Drew."

"Me, too. I'm sure he's really disappointed. We do everything together."

"Even if you both went to the Camporee, you wouldn't be in the same cadre."

"Probably not." Adam glanced over his shoulder. "Actually, I'm kind of looking forward to doing something on my own."

I'd always thought it'd be cool to do everything with a brother close to my own age. But maybe I'd get sick of spending as much time together as those two did. "I can see that."

Just then Drew came out the door. He glanced at us, but hurried to the DeWitts' Suburban waiting on the corner with its motor running.

Adam walked after him. "See you Sunday."

CAMPOREE ROADBLOCKS

On the walk home after Cadets, the snow crunched under my shoes and the cold air froze my nose hairs. The light above the sink shone in a bright square on our driveway. I hoped Luke was in bed. And that I wouldn't have to sleep with him.

When I came in, the den lamp glowed on a pile of stuff on the couch. I walked over. My pajamas and my pillow topped a stack of sheets and blankets.

Good old Dad talked Mom into it.

The steps creaked. John walked into the kitchen and opened the refrigerator. "Hey, bro. How was Cadets?"

"Okay." I hung up my coat. "We got information about Camporee."

"Yeah?" John dug through the fruit in the crisper drawer. "When is it?"

"The end of July. In some place that sounds kind of like Canada—" I picked up my *Crusader* and checked the cover. "Oh, yeah. Kamp Kananaskis. It's in Alberta."

"In the mountains?"

"Sure thing." I spread a sheet on the couch.

John came into the den, munching an apple. "Let me see." He picked up my *Crusader*.

"That's mine." I lunged for it. "It has information I need."

"Relax." He lifted it high, out of my reach. "I'm just looking at it."

"Well, don't. Not with sticky fingers." I swung to grab the magazine, but missed.

"My fingers aren't sticky. I'm not messy like Luke."

"Yeah, and you're not a restless sleeper either, but you won't share a room with me."

"At least you get to camp down here now."

"Yeah. Dad must have talked Mom into it." I held out my hand. "Give me my magazine."

"In a minute." John sat in Dad's recliner. "I want to look at the Camporee information."

An icy fist grabbed my heart. "Why?"

"Going to the mountains would be so much better than boring old Michigan."

The fist squeezed. "But you're too old to go."

"Maybe as a Cadet." He flipped open the magazine. "But I could be a junior counselor."

"Are you crazy?"

"No, it'd be fun." He stared at a page. "Sweet. The junior counselors get to go white-water rafting."

"What of it? You've already gone to Camporee. It's my turn now."

"I can go if I want to."

Dad's study door opened and he strode into the den. "What's going on here?" He crossed his arms. "You guys are going to wake up Luke if you don't quiet down."

"Trust me, Dad." I shook my head. "It would take a lot more than this to wake him up."

"What are you two arguing about?"

"John has my *Crusader* and won't give it back."

John shrugged. "I'm just looking at it."

"I don't want him to touch it while he's eating an apple." I pointed. "He might get it sticky and I need to read all the information about Camporee."

"Simmer down, Matt." Dad stared at John. "Give him back his *Crusader.*"

"Sure." John tossed me the magazine. "I was just headed upstairs anyway." He stood and turned his back to Dad. Then he scowled at me.

Dad's voice rose. "That's enough, John."

I stared at Dad in surprise. How could he have known what John was doing?

John looked surprised, too, but just for a second. Then he shrugged. "Okay." He took a big bite out of his apple and strolled up the stairs.

"Thanks, Dad." I laid my *Crusader* on the table. "And thanks for letting me sleep here."

"Don't thank me. You'll have to thank your mother. She's the one willing to do extra laundry so you can avoid drool-in-mouth syndrome."

"I'll go tell her right now."

"I suggest waiting 'til morning. She's already in bed."

"Okay." I spread a top sheet over the one already on the couch.

"You know, Matt, sleeping here is conditional."

"Conditional?"

"As long as you meet the condition of putting away your bedding each morning, you can keep sleeping here. But if you don't put it away, you're back upstairs."

"Even if I forget just one time?"

"You're old enough to remember on your own. Mom doesn't need the extra stress of reminding you every morning. It's your choice to keep sleeping here or not."

"Okay. I'll remember."

Dad started down the hall. "Hey, Dad." I picked up my *Crusader*. "The Camporee will be in the mountains. In Canada."

"Oh, that sounds like such fun."

"I can't wait. Here, let me show you the picture."

I opened the magazine to the picture of the mountains and the moon and handed it to him.

He whistled softly. "Beautiful. Makes you want to hop a plane and take off, doesn't it?"

"That's just what I'll do." I picked up a blanket. "We're going to fly from Des Moines to Calgary."

"That should be fun. You've never flown before."

"I know. It will be awesome." I snapped the blanket open and let it fall over the sheet. "Only it's going to be kind of expensive."

"How expensive?"

"Hawkeye Council will pay half the registration fee."

"That should help. What's our share?"

"It will be $80."

"That's not so bad."

"But there's also transportation expense." I slowly fluffed my pillow. "Part of the transportation cost is due by February 15."

"How much?"

"Mr. Flanders said $120."

"And that's only part of the transportation cost?"

"Yeah."

"How much is the full expense?"

"They don't know for sure yet—"

"Well, do they have an idea?"

"They think maybe around $450."

"Did you say $450? That's a lot of money, Matthew, especially if you add the registration fee to it. Then it comes to over $500."

"Only $200 is due by February 15, the rest can be paid later."

"That will help, but it's still expensive."

"I know."

"Mom and I will have to talk this over, Matt." Dad sighed. "I'm just not sure we can swing this right now."

"But this is my only chance for Camporee, Dad. John got to go when he was my age."

"You're right, Matt, he did go to Camporee—"

"It's my turn now," I interrupted. "I've been wanting to go for three years."

Dad rubbed my hair. "I know how important this is to you, Matt. And I believe Camporee is a great experience. But we just don't have hundreds of extra dollars lying around and we have some other expenses coming up—"

"Like a new baby." I sighed.

"Right." Dad rubbed his late-night stubble. "We'll have doctor bills and things we need to buy before the baby's born. And more expenses after the baby arrives."

"I get that, Dad. But Camporee only comes around every three years."

Dad hugged me. "We'll see what we can do." Then he went upstairs.

I put on my pajamas, shut off the lamp, and crawled between the sheets.

What if Mom and Dad don't let me go? What if they can't afford it? What if John messes it up for me by asking to go as a junior counselor?

I opened my *Crusader* and stared at the picture of the mountains in the dim light. It seemed like I was on a helicopter that was slowly flying farther and farther and farther away.

OPPOSITION MOUNTS

I woke to cabinets clicking and water running. In the kitchen, Dad filled the coffeepot under a streaming faucet. I'd had no clue making coffee was so noisy.

Maybe if I put my blankets away quickly, I could catch Dad in a good mood and discuss Camporee again. Maybe during the night he'd figured out a way to pay for it.

Luke came down and whined for a glass of milk. Dad made him ask nicely and sit at the table. Just as I tossed my pillow on the stack in the closet, something crashed.

When I rushed into the kitchen, I saw Luke's glass had shattered. Sharp shards lay on the table, while milk spread across it and dribbled onto the floor.

"Oh, Luke!" Dad leaped forward. "I told you to sit still. Now look what you've done."

He snatched a kitchen towel and threw it on the table. Then he grabbed another and squatted on the floor to wipe up the widening white pool.

I bunched the towel on the table into a barrier to keep more milk from dripping off. I frowned and muttered, "Way to go, Luke."

Luke began blubbering.

Dad dropped his dripping towel into the sink. "Hush up, Luke." He grabbed a paper napkin and shoved the chunks of broken glass into the wastebasket. He wiped up the sticky milk with more towels and washed the table. Then he jerked open a drawer and smacked two spoons on the damp table.

This was not the time to bring up Camporee.

While Luke and I ate cold cereal, Dad rinsed and squeezed the dirty towels. As soon as we finished, he told us to get dressed. "No funny business." He wrapped a dry towel around the soggy ones and headed downstairs with the bundle. "I don't want you disturbing your mother."

By the time we came back into the kitchen, Dad had started the washing machine and mopped the floor. He finally poured himself his first cup of coffee.

"Get on your coats and boots, guys." He took a tiny sip. "And make it fast. I've got work I should be doing."

As we walked to the bus stop, I thought I'd try to talk to Dad that evening. Maybe by then, he and Mom would have come up with a Camporee plan.

But right after dinner, the phone rang in Dad's study. He had a long conversation, and then he asked Mom to come in. I couldn't understand a word of their murmurs. But when they came out, they both looked worried.

It wouldn't do to mention Camporee. If I asked while they were in a bad mood, they just might say no. And that would be the end of my Camporee dream.

I quickly finished my homework so I could read *Lost in Manhattan*. It was too suspenseful to put down, and I finished it before bedtime.

On Friday evening, Dad took two more calls in his study and came out frowning after each one. I decided to wait until another day. I started *Prince Caspian*, and read about how the Pevensie children were pulled into another land.

Saturday morning Mom made Luke dust while I vacuumed. She walked toward the front door and motioned for me to shut off the Hoover. Someone must have rung the bell. I heard the study door close.

Mom glanced at us. "Go ahead with your work."

I finished the den and shut off the machine. Whoever was in the study with Dad was talking very loudly.

Mom hurried into the den. "You two go upstairs and clean your room."

I pulled the vacuum up each step, and Luke followed with the dust cloth.

In our room, he whined about missing cartoons, so I promised he could play with my Legos as soon as he finished dusting. We cleaned in record time. Then I hurried down, bumping the vacuum along behind me.

Before I got to the bottom, the front door slammed. It didn't sound like our visitor left in a good mood.

On my way to put the vacuum in the back closet, I took the scenic route through the living room. I peered between the curtains and saw Mr. Baker get into his old pickup. I hurried to the closet and shoved the vacuum beside the winter coats. Why was Mr. Baker so upset?

Dad came into the kitchen and helped himself to coffee. Then he stared out the window. I had a feeling it wouldn't be smart to ask about Camporee now.

He noticed me. "Did you clean your room?"

"Yes, sir." I snapped a salute, but he didn't even smile.

He sipped and looked at me over his cup rim. "Then you're free to do what you want."

I went upstairs to read more in *Prince Caspian*. The Pevensies had discovered a treasure cave and finally

realized they were back in Narnia. I was sure they'd have
some exciting adventures. I picked up the book and
relaxed on the bed.

Luke looked up from playing with my Legos. "Hey, get
off my bed."

"It's my bed, too."

"Not anymore. You don't want to share with me, so
it's my bed now."

He was being noisy anyway. I took *Prince Caspian*
downstairs and got comfortable on the den couch.
Enough light came from the kitchen that I didn't bother
to turn on the lamp.

My parents were talking in the study. As they walked
into the kitchen, Dad shook his head. "I just don't
understand such opposition."

"I don't either, honey. Let's hope not too many other
people feel the same."

"This is crazy. Do they think they can stay forever in
that dinky little building?"

"Some of them have attended that church all their
lives." Mom put a hand on Dad's arm. "The building
itself carries a lot of emotional freight for them."

"But that's just it. It's only a building." Dad ran his
fingers through his hair. "Maybe I should preach a
sermon on idolizing objects."

"When you were in seminary," she reached up and
adjusted his collar, "you asked me to remind you never
to preach sermons aimed at people who disagreed with
you."

"Did I?"

"Yes." She twined her hands around his neck. "So I'm reminding you."

"Thanks. I think." Dad's arms wrapped around her waist.

"It won't bother you so much tomorrow. We just have to keep praying."

"Amen and amen to that, sister." Dad lowered his head and kissed her on the lips—for a long time. I scrunched down and held my book in front of my face.

When I came into the house after piano lessons that afternoon, Luke messed with yellow Play-Doh on the kitchen table. Making smashing noises, he pounded the blob into a pancake. Then he made motor sounds while rolling the disk back into a ball.

I helped myself to a glass of milk.

Luke made squeaking noises, lifting the ball with a stiff arm like a crane. He dropped it with a splashing sound. Then he squished it while making spitty noises.

I rolled my eyes. "Can't you shape something?"

"Like what?"

"I don't know. Maybe an animal of some kind."

Luke's forehead wrinkled. "Like a bunny or a doggie?"

"Sure."

He shook his head. "The machines are moving dirt."

"Well, cut out all the sound effects."

Motor mouth continued his excavations.

I found *Prince Caspian* in the den and went up to our room. I lay on the bed and opened the book. Trumpkin the dwarf was telling the children about Prince Caspian and his evil uncle.

"Hey, little brother." John stood with one hand grasping the door frame, scowling at me.

"Yeah?"

"You been in my room again?"

"No, why?"

"I'm missing a book. You sure you didn't sneak into my room?"

"I'm sure." I sat up. "I haven't been in your room and I didn't take your book."

"It's one of the Space Trilogy books." He stalked into the room and peered around. "Have you got it here somewhere?"

"I said I didn't take it." I pointed to the page I'd been reading. "I've got my own books to read. Which I'm trying to do now, if you get my drift."

"I get your drift all right." John moved closer to the bed. "But you've snuck into my room before and messed with my books. Why should I believe you now?"

"Because I'm telling the truth, that's why." I snapped *Prince Caspian* shut. "Besides, I was the one who asked Dad to buy those books for you."

"Right." John narrowed his eyes. "And why did you ask him to buy them? Because you wanted to read them, too?"

"Oh, give me a break." I swung my feet onto the floor. "I was trying to be nice, for crying out loud."

"I'll give you a break that'll make you cry out loud." John shook a fist. "If I find you've been lying to me."

"I'm not lying!" I jumped up. "Why don't you just leave my room and leave me alone?"

He clenched his hands. "I'll go when I'm good and ready."

"Just like you'll do everything whenever you want." I jabbed my finger on his chest. "Just like you'll go to Camporee, even when it's my turn!"

John took a small step back. "I can be a junior counselor if I want to."

"What's going on here?" Mom stood in the doorway, holding a basket of folded laundry. John didn't say a thing. I didn't say anything either.

She stepped into the room. "I asked you two what's going on."

"Nothing." John crossed his arms. "I just wondered if Matt borrowed one of my books."

"Which I didn't."

Mom sighed and walked toward us. "I thought you two were making an effort to get along better." She set the basket on the bed.

John said, "Tell him to stay out of my room."

I pointed at him. "Who's in whose room?"

"Enough." Mom pulled out a stack of clothes. "John, these are yours. Put them away."

John grabbed his laundry and left.

"Okay, Matt." Mom motioned me over. "Find your clothes and put them away."

I put my stuff in my drawers while Mom put Luke's in his. Then she sat on the bed.

"Now." She looked in my eyes. "Tell me what the problem is this time."

"John thinks I took a book, which I didn't." No way would I mention his crazy idea about going to Camporee.

"Doesn't he believe you?"

"No."

Mom put a hand on my shoulder. "I guess you'll just have to make sure you're a person of your word, so that John believes the things you say."

"I'm trying, Mom. It's John that's the problem."

"I know you're making an effort, Matt." Mom gently squeezed my shoulder. "But try thinking less about how John acts toward you and more about how you act toward him."

I frowned at the floor and shrugged off her hand. Then I picked up my book.

She stood. "What are you reading?"

"*Prince Caspian.*"

"How far are you?"

"Trumpkin the dwarf thinks the children won't be any help in a battle."

"Oh, what happens next is one of my favorite parts."

"Yeah?"

"Yes, but I won't give it away." She picked up the empty basket. "I'll let you read it for yourself." Then she left the room.

I lay back down on the bed and opened my book. But the words blurred on the page. I kept replaying what Mom had said about John and me.

Lord, help me be truthful all the time so that John will believe what I say. And help me be a nicer brother. And please let me go to Camporee.

CHURCH MOUSE

Every morning I folded my sheets and blankets and put them in the hall closet. I never felt like it, but I did it anyway. Anything to avoid sleeping with Luke, the human water faucet.

And every afternoon, I practiced piano for a half hour. There were lots of things I'd rather do, but each time I practiced without being told, I earned a point with Mom.

And I needed all the points I could get. Because whenever I asked my parents about Camporee, their non-answer was always, "We're thinking about it."

On the day of the congregational meeting, I was in my room after dinner, reading about how the children and Trumpkin planned to find Caspian.

"Hey." John came into my room. "Do you think the proposal will pass?"

"I hope so." I put a bookmark in my place. "I can't wait to move to a bigger house and have my own room."

"I hope we move, too, but I don't think everyone likes the proposal."

"Do you suppose that's why Dad's been taking so many calls in his study?"

"I guess so. He doesn't seem very happy lately."

"Mom either." She was probably worried about how we'd fit another kid into our already-crowded house.

John looked out my window at the church. "I sure would like to be a mouse at that meeting tonight."

"But Mom and Dad are going." I joined him. "So we have to make sure Luke goes to bed on time."

"Yeah." John shrugged. "We'll just have to wait until they get home to find out what happens." He walked out.

I stared at the church. The building was dark against the dusky sky, but someone had turned on the lights and the stained glass windows glowed like bright jewels. John was right. A mouse could hide inside without being seen and hear every word.

Still carrying *Prince Caspian*, I went to John's room. He was reading, but quickly closed the book and shoved it under his pillow.

I wrinkled my forehead. "What were you reading?"

"Nothing."

"Come on, John. I saw you push that book under your pillow. Why are you hiding it? Is it a dirty book or something?"

"Of course not."

"What then?"

John's face turned red. He reached beneath his pillow and pulled out the book.

I twisted my head to try to read the title. "It's from the Space Trilogy, isn't it?"

"Yeah."

"Oh, I get it. It's the one you lost. The one you thought I took."

"Right. Sorry about that, bro."

"I figured you'd find it sooner or later. Where was it?"

"Beneath my bed. I must have laid it on the floor and kicked it under accidentally. I'm sorry I accused you of snooping in my room and taking my book."

"It's okay. Forget it." I waved my hand. "But there's another thing I'd like you to forget."

"What's that?"

"Forget about going to Camporee." I touched my chest. "I still don't know if I can go. Every time I ask, Mom and Dad say they're still thinking about it."

"They *are* taking a really long time to decide." John flipped open the book and turned to his page. "I'll give that serious consideration."

"Thanks." I stopped by his door and glanced back. "I'm going for a walk."

"Fine." He didn't even look up.

My parents' bedroom door was open a crack, and I heard my name. I stopped to listen.

"I think we should try to scrape the money together," Dad said. "We let John go."

"But that was in Michigan, and the transportation costs weren't nearly as high."

They're talking about sending me to Camporee.

"It helps that they're breaking up the payments."

Mom's voice was sad. "It's still a lot of money."

"I know." Their closet door thunked shut. "But it's a great experience for a growing boy."

"We have a little time. Let's give it more thought."

I trotted down the steps. *Mom and Dad are thinking about Camporee, John's thinking about Camporee, and I'm thinking about Camporee. Oh, Lord, please work it out so I can go.* Then I added, *If it's your will, that is.*

Zombie Luke stared at a Transformers video in the den. I quietly took my coat from the closet, slid my arms into the sleeves, and picked up my book. I slipped through the back door and gently pulled it shut with an almost silent click.

The church door was unlocked and swung open with a long squeak. I paused to listen for anyone coming, but only the furnace fan echoed in the quiet building. The lights above the staircase were off, so climbing the creaky steps in the dark was spooky. The balcony lights weren't on either, but the sanctuary lights made it bright enough to read. I crept to the front of the balcony and squatted beside its low wall. I folded my coat into a thick cushion on the floor and sat on it. No one could see me.

I opened *Prince Caspian* and read about how Trumpkin and the children rowed their boat all day.

Downstairs, doors opened and closed. People talked and sometimes laughed. I yawned. I spread out my coat and rolled the hood into a pillow. I curled up on it and started reading again. Lucy walked through the woods at night, speaking to the trees and trying to wake them.

The trees murmured. One tree morphed into an old man and started talking loudly.

I opened my eyes. The wood in front of me was not a beech tree in the moonlight, but a church bench in a dim balcony. Someone spoke loudly in the sanctuary below. I must have fallen asleep and the congregational meeting had already started.

I peeked over the balcony railing. It was Mr. Baker. "I have worshiped in this building for eighty-three years. Before I could walk, my father carried me here in his arms. I met and married my wife in this church. This is where all our children were baptized and professed their faith in Jesus Christ. We have a rich heritage here. We don't need a different building."

He sat down. Mr. Beyer, Mr. Tom Loursma, and Mr. Walters sat at a table in front of the pulpit. Mr. Beyer said, "Yes, Mr. Thomason?"

My catechism teacher got up. "I want to thank the Committee for coming up with this fine proposal." He held out both hands. "We all know the situation. We have too little space for too many people. We have fifth graders traipsing through the pastor's home on Sundays. We're packed like sardines at every service."

A little laughter rippled through the audience.

"I respect the former speaker's sentiments," he went on. "We do, indeed, have a rich heritage of teaching and preaching in this place. And we've seen God's mercy to continuing generations. But we don't lose these things by simply changing buildings." He thumped his fist on the back of the pew in front of him. "This building is not the church." A few people clapped.

"The Lord has providentially provided a 'win-win-win' solution. We secure the space we need. Celebration Church sells their old property and pays some of their debt. The E Free church gets a building of their own and a home for their pastor. It's a threefold blessing for three congregations. Thank you, Mr. Chairman."

People clapped as he sat.

Mr. Beyer nodded at another man. "Mr. Kroninga."

Mr. Kroninga stood with some papers in his hand. "As Chairman of the Youth Education Committee, I'd like to share a few statistics with the congregation." He shuffled the papers. "We've been outgrowing this building ever since Reverend Vos arrived." He glanced down and read. "The number of children undergoing instruction in our congregation has doubled in the last seven years. In the last three years, we've baptized thirty-one babies." He looked up. "People, where are we going to put all these kids when they start attending Sunday school?"

He sat down to loud applause.

Mr. Cummings spoke next. "It's true we've been outgrowing this building since Reverend Vos arrived. But pastors come and pastors go, don't they? Someday he'll leave. Then our congregation might dwindle again. Why saddle future generations with a heavy load of debt when this building would have been perfectly adequate?"

A few people clapped as he sat down.

Mr. Beyer rubbed his forehead. "Mr. Dennison."

I sat up straighter. Mr. Dennison looked really old. He grasped the pew ahead of him and pulled himself up. "Mr. Chairman, fathers and brothers—and sisters." He nodded at the people in the pews. "I would like to say that we need to keep in mind our Lord's teaching concerning the subject of debt. In Romans 13:8, the apostle Paul writes, 'Let no debt remain outstanding, except the continuing debt to love one another—'"

Mr. Dennison went on and on, quoting Scripture and saying it was wrong to get into debt. Some people whispered to each other. I heard a soft laugh in the back.

What time is it getting to be? John will be sure to have missed me by now. Mom might even run home and check if Luke is getting to bed on time.

I slipped on my coat, picked up my book, and felt my way down the dark steps.

On the landing, I peered around the corner. No one stood in the back of church. I stood quietly for a minute, listening for doors opening or footsteps, but didn't hear anything. I dashed down the rest of the stairs and out the door. Then I ran all the way home.

"Where have you been?" John yelled the minute I stepped through the back door. "I was about ready to call the police and file a missing person's report."

"At the congregational meeting." I hung up my coat.

"Yeah? What happened?"

I told him who had spoken for the proposal and who had spoken against it. "I split while Mr. Dennison was talking. I didn't want to chance Mom coming home and catching me out."

"No worries," John said. "Luke has been tucked into his little bed."

"That's still my little bed, too." I shook my head sadly.

"At least you're sleeping in the den now."

"But it's a pain to put away that stuff every morning and make my bed every night. I could move in with you."

"No, you can't. My room and bed are even smaller." John pulled two glasses from the cabinet. "Besides, maybe we'll all be moving soon and you can have your own room." He took the milk jug from the fridge. "So you didn't hear how the vote went?"

"No, I didn't dare stay any longer."

"Luke was worried about you. You better go up and say good night to him if he's still awake." He poured milk into the glasses.

"I'll do that." I headed up the steps.

John called softly behind me. "Then come down and tell me more about the meeting."

29

ANSWERS AND QUESTIONS

When I heard Mom put a pan on the stove the next morning, I threw off my covers and stumbled into the kitchen. "What happened at the meeting?"

"Dad will tell you all about it when everybody's here." She broke an egg into the pan. "Please get out the juice and put it on the table." She picked up another egg.

Dad came down the steps, leading Luke by the hand. John followed. When they were in the kitchen, Dad dropped Luke's hand. "I'm sure you're all wondering about the results of the meeting last night." He sighed. "Only sixty-two percent of the people voted in favor of the Building and Grounds proposal."

"Sixty-two percent?" John plopped on his chair. "Well, that's a majority, right?"

"Not as much as the council would like." Dad poured juice into my glass. "We knew a unanimous vote wasn't possible, but we'd hoped for about seventy-five percent."

My hands trembled as I pulled out my chair. Wasn't I going to get my own room? Would I have to go back to sleeping with Luke? I sat and stared at the moisture condensing on my cold glass.

"But, Dad." John's forehead wrinkled. "Does it matter how the people vote? Haven't you always said that the council—not the congregation—makes the decisions?"

"That's true." Dad poured juice for Luke. "But it wouldn't be wise to undertake a large financial obligation without support from most of the people."

I looked up. "Why not?"

"The people in the congregation are the ones who have to be willing to open not only their minds to the project, but also their checkbooks." Dad sighed as he set down the juice carton. "The council's not going forward with the plan at this point."

"But we need a bigger house." I crossed my arms. "It's not fair."

"What may not be fair in this situation is to expect almost half the people in the congregation to help pay for a project they voted against." Dad tapped the table in front of me. "There's more at stake here than you having your own room, Matthew Henry Vos."

I bit my lip. With the tip of my finger, I wrote in the moisture on my glass, "NOT FAIR!"

"The Council met briefly after the meeting." Dad combed his fingers through his hair. "We decided not to pursue this proposal now, but we'll discuss it more at our next meeting."

Mom dropped the spoon she'd been using to stir the eggs and sat down. She pushed away her plate and laid her head on the table. She'd have yelled at me if I'd put my head on a set table.

Dad patted her arm. "Don't worry, honey." He went to the stove. "I'll handle the eggs."

John frowned. "What's the matter, Mom?"

Mom lifted her head to look at John and then at Dad.

Dad nodded while he stirred. "I think it's time."

Mom sat up straight and took a deep breath. "Our family is about to become larger." She smiled around at us. "I'm pregnant."

John pulled back his head and arched his eyebrows. "You're kidding."

I grinned. "Cool."

Luke scrunched up his face. "Huh?"

Mom patted Luke's head. "I'm going to have a baby."

"A baby boy or a baby girl?"

"We don't know." Dad turned off the burner. "What we do know is that you'll be a big brother."

"Me? A big brother?" Luke's eyes got wide.

"That's right, kiddo." Dad brought the pan to the table. "You're going to have to be a big boy and help Mom take care of the baby."

"When I ask you," Mom added quickly.

"All of you need to help her out as much as possible from now on." Dad scraped some eggs onto Luke's plate. "Especially since she hasn't been feeling very well."

John frowned. "Who knows about this?"

Mom pointed. "You three are the first to know."

Dad and I looked at each other. He quickly spooned a helping of eggs onto my plate.

I asked, "May I tell my friends?"

John rolled his eyes. "Why would you want to?"

I didn't bother to answer.

Dad sat down. "Let's pray." He prayed for a blessing on the food and asked God to grant the council guidance about the proposal. Then he thanked God for this gift of new life and asked that he help us all rejoice in it.

I ate my eggs before they got any colder. "My Cadet counselor asked last week if I've sent in my registration form and fees. He'll probably ask about it again tonight."

Mom looked at me. "When is that due?"

Before I could answer, Dad spoke. "February 15."

Mom glanced at the calendar. "We have two more weeks then." She looked worried. "We'll give it some more thought."

Dad apparently decided it was time to change the subject. "What's been happening at school lately, boys?"

John grunted. "Not much."

I shrugged. "Same here."

"I didn't go to school yesterday." Luke sputtered yellow chewed eggs. "I go today."

Dad didn't give up. "How about you, John? What did you find most interesting yesterday?"

"Oh, that was definitely biology. We dissected a frog."

"Matt." Mom quickly set down her juice glass. "Let's hear your most interesting thing."

It had been a pretty boring day, except for science. "I guess science class."

Mom tilted her head. "I didn't think that was one of your favorite subjects."

"It's not."

Dad smiled. "What happened to make it interesting?"

"We talked about how it took billions of years for man to develop from apes."

John snorted. "Ha!"

Luke's face scrunched up again. "Apes?"

"It's just something some people think," Dad told him. "It's not what the Bible teaches."

I remembered every word from class. "Mr. Bates asked me what I thought about that."

Dad said, "But he knows you're a creationist—"

"Yeah, he knows."

"How did you answer him?"

"That the Bible says God created man from the dust of the earth."

"And?"

"He said, 'The body is more than sixty percent water, so you're saying that we're nothing more than mud?'"

"What did you say then?"

"I said we were a lot more important than mud because God breathed the breath of life into the first man and he became a living soul."

"How did he respond?"

"He just said, 'Well, you're certainly entitled to your own opinion.' And then he told the class how man gradually evolved and got less hair and began standing more upright. He showed us a time line with pictures and everything."

Dad frowned. "Did anyone else speak up?"

"Get real, Dad." John shrugged. "You think those kids are going to open themselves up to ridicule in class? They may not agree with the teacher, but they're not going to say anything."

"No one else." I sighed. "But afterward Mike said he agreed with me. Later in the cafeteria, Jessica and Angela stopped by my table and thanked me for telling the truth."

"I admire you for telling the truth, too." Dad smiled at me. "I'm sure it wasn't easy."

I didn't like Dad saying he admired me. If Mr. Bates hadn't asked me, I wouldn't have said a peep.

"I wonder—" Dad stared above my head.

John asked, "What?"

"I just had a brainwave." Dad lifted his coffee cup. "But I'll keep it to myself for now."

After breakfast, Dad left his dishes on the table and went into his study.

As I folded my sheets and blankets, I heard him talking on the phone. "Ralph, let's invite the Youth Education Committee to our meeting next week."

I brought the pile of bedding down the hall and opened the closet. Dad spoke to Mr. Beyer again. "You know that idea you and I have kicked around, but always dismissed as impractical?" There was a brief pause.

"Yep, that's the one." Another pause.

"Exactly what I thought. Let's see what the Committee thinks." Pause. "Okay, we'll talk more later." Dad hung up and walked out of his study.

I quickly tossed in my bedding. "What was that all about, Dad?"

He rubbed my hair. "You know better than to ask about calls I make in the study." He gave me a little punch on my shoulder. "And you know better than to eavesdrop, too."

30

DELAYS

Someone spoke, but the voice was muffled. I pulled the covers off my head and blinked.

Dad smiled at me. "Good morning, Matt."

"Morning, Dad. What time is it?"

"It's almost 7:30."

"Seven thirty!" I sat up. "We missed the bus!"

"Don't worry. School is delayed two hours because the roads are icy."

"Oh, good. Then we've got lots of time." I lay back on my pillow.

"Well, you may want to get up." Dad smacked his hands together. "Because I've got a blueberry pancake with your name on it."

I jumped up to put away my stuff. When I came into the kitchen, Dad flipped a pancake. He didn't just turn it over, like Mom would have done, but he actually tossed it into the air.

I held my breath. He moved the pan a bit and caught it. I exhaled. "Can you teach me to do that, Dad?"

"Sure. You can help me make a couple. After you eat this." He slid the pancake onto a plate and handed it to me. "Say your prayers and dig in."

I closed my eyes, folded my hands, and prayed. *Lord, thank you for this blueberry pancake and please let me go to Camporee, for Jesus' sake, Amen.*

When I opened my eyes, I saw an "M" in the middle of my pancake. "You weren't kidding." I traced the letter with syrup. "It really does have my name on it."

"Your initial anyway." Dad poured batter into the pan.

By the time Luke stumbled into the kitchen, Dad had a smiley face pancake ready for him. And I'd finished my "M" one. I joined Dad by the stove. "Can you teach me how to flip now?"

"You bet. Got an idea for a design?"

"What about a knight's shield?"

He showed me how to drip a thin stream of batter into a shield shape. Then he poured more batter over it. He pointed to the outside edge of the pancake. "Wait to turn it until these bubbles form little holes." When the tiny holes were firm, he slid his turner under the pancake. "Make sure it's not stuck to the pan."

"Then you flip it?"

"Yep." He winked at me. "It's all in the wrist." I held the pan's handle and he put his hand around mine. We lifted the pan and gave it a jerk. The pancake twisted into the air, and we lunged forward, catching it as it fell.

"Perfecto!" Dad grinned. "Now just give it a minute to brown on that side, and it's ready to eat."

While I ate it, he made Luke's second one with a number "5" on it, pointing out that some numbers and letters needed to be written backward. I made my third pancake into a pirate face with an eye patch. And I flipped and caught it by myself!

While Luke and I ate, Dad made a few more pancakes and put them on a platter. Luke pushed away his plate with half a pancake still on it. "I'm full."

"That's a perfectly good pancake." I pointed with my fork. "You can't let it go to waste."

"I don't want it."

Dad looked at me. "You want to finish it?"

"And get Luke germs? No way."

"Okay." Dad brought the platter to the table and sat. "I'll eat it."

I thought I'd gag. "Gross!"

"I don't think Luke's germs will kill me."

"I wouldn't be so sure."

He pulled Luke's syrupy plate toward him. "Don't worry, I won't use his fork."

"Good thing. If you did, you'd never get it unstuck from your hand."

Dad chuckled. "Have you had enough to eat?"

"I think so." The steaming stack of pancakes smelled good, but my stomach was almost as full as it'd been at Mr. Houser's. "I suppose I should save some for John."

"John's snooze alarm has gone off three times, and I've called him twice." Dad stabbed Luke's pancake with his own fork. "He's not having breakfast today unless he makes it himself."

I made a mental note never to ignore Dad's calls.

"What about Mommy?" Luke tried to wipe his hands with his napkin, but all he managed to do was rip the paper into shreds that clung to his fingers. "Doesn't she get any pancakes?"

"Mommy's not hungry right now." Dad speared the last square of pancake from Luke's plate. "She's going to rest a little longer this morning."

Luke looked at Dad with big eyes. "Is the baby making her sick again?"

"She isn't feeling well." Dad leaned toward Luke. "But the baby isn't making her sick."

My stomach lurched as if a river rock had dropped into it. "What's wrong with Mom now?"

"Nothing." Dad shook his head. "It's just morning sickness from being pregnant, but I don't want Luke to blame the baby."

I sighed with relief. "Yeah, I guess it's not the baby's fault. He can't help it."

"He or she." Dad swung his fork from side to side in the air to remind me of the two options. "We don't know which it is yet."

Luke pressed sticky hands against the table edge and pushed back his chair. "I want a little brother to play trains with me."

"The baby won't be able to play with you for a long time." Dad helped himself to more pancakes. "At first it will be so small that he—or she—won't be able to walk or talk. The baby will mostly just eat and sleep."

Luke wrinkled his forehead. "The baby will just eat and sleep?"

"We certainly hope so." Dad drizzled syrup over his pancakes.

Luke hopped off his chair. "What a boring baby!"

"That's the best kind." I picked up my dirty dishes. "If they're eating or sleeping, they're not bawling their lungs out or breaking your toys."

Dad folded his hands. "Before you guys take off, let's pray together."

Luke extended his arms. "Can we hold hands?"

"May we hold hands." Dad looked at the shreds of napkin dangling from Luke's sticky fingers. "Not this morning. And you'd better wash yours immediately after prayer. Do not touch anything on the way to the bathroom. Do not pass Go. Do not collect $200."

Luke's forehead wrinkled again. "$200?"

I rolled my eyes. "It's from Monopoly."

After Luke left to wash up, Dad and I were alone. This might be a good time to mention the Camporee. I cleared my throat. "You know, Dad, we're getting close to the deadline for Camporee registration."

"I know." Dad's forehead wrinkled now. "It's the fifteenth, isn't it?"

"Yes, February 15, only a week from tomorrow. My Cadet counselor will probably ask me again tonight if I've sent in my forms."

"Mom and I have been discussing it."

I tried to keep my voice calm. "You've been talking about it for a long time."

"I know, Matt." Dad put down his fork and sighed. "But before we send off your registration, we have to pay some bills and figure out our account balance."

My voice shook. "How long will that take?"

Dad frowned. "I'm not really sure. Mom usually pays the bills, but she hasn't been keeping on top of things very well lately."

"We only have a week!"

"I'll go over the bills with Mom in the next day or two." Dad looked into my eyes. "But it's more than just the $200. We have to come up with $500 all together."

"I know it's expensive, but that's because we're flying to Calgary to camp in the mountains." I took a deep breath. "I've never even seen mountains."

"It will be a great experience, I'm sure." Dad still stared at my face. "And not just because you'll fly and see mountains for the first time. You'll practice new skills, meet new people, and learn more about God and his creation. Those are more important reasons for going to Camporee. Do you understand?"

"Sure, I get it."

"Good." He gently tapped his fist under my chin. "Mom and I will get things figured out and make a decision soon. Okay?"

"Okay, Dad."

How would Mom and Dad ever come up with an extra $500 after they paid all their bills? Especially with baby expenses coming up. Maybe I wouldn't get to fly on a jet and camp in the mountains. By the time the next Camporee came around, I'd be too old. Unless I pulled a John and went as a junior counselor. But even then, I wouldn't be in the mountains.

OH, BROTHER!

I put my shoes in my backpack so Drill Sergeant Griswold wouldn't have a reason to yell at me during PE. Then I stuffed in my homework.

Dad came out of his study. "Ready for school?"

"Yep."

He glanced at his watch. "What're you going to do now?"

"Maybe get piano practice out of the way."

"Great idea." Dad called up the stairs. "Luke? Where are you? Time to get dressed."

"I'm here."

Dad and I followed Luke's voice into the living room, but I didn't see my little brother.

Dad looked around. "Where?"

"Here." It came from the window. Luke's red pajama feet showed under the curtains.

Dad jerked a drape open. "Luke! Why are you coloring on the window?"

Unbelievable, but true. Luke held a crayon in his hand, coloring on the glass. He smiled. "I'm making pretty pictures on the window, like Jenny's house."

Dad stared at him. "What?"

It came to me in a flash. "Jenny stuck Valentine's Day cling-ons to their front window."

"Oh." Dad pulled Luke from between the curtains. "Jenny used plastic pictures, Luke. That stick on windows and peel off easily. Crayons are for coloring books, *not* for windows."

Dad turned toward me. "Matt, get the Windex and bring a roll of paper towels."

After I handed the stuff to Dad, he sprayed the marks. Luke immediately screamed. "Don't ruin it, Daddy!"

"We have to clean it, Luke." Dad was amazingly calm. "You are not supposed to color on the window. Here." He handed him a paper towel. "Scrub it."

I tore a towel from the roll and helped rub. Nobody ever had to tell me not to color on windows. Not even when I was a lot younger than Luke.

The red marks came off easily, which was good because Luke had drawn a lot of hearts. We scrubbed harder to get off the purple and blue shapes, but the yellow and green squiggles stuck like glue.

Dad touched Luke's shoulder. "Stay here." He went to the bathroom and came back with a razor blade from his shaver. He sprayed Windex on the stubborn marks. Then he scraped them with his razor blade. Finally he wiped off the crayon flecks with a paper towel.

"There." Dad stood back and examined the window. "I don't think even your mother will see anything. Luke, throw away those dirty towels. Then you and I are going upstairs to get you dressed for school."

Dad patted my head. "Thanks for your help, Matt."

As Dad put away the razor blade, I heard him mutter, "So much for sermon preparation this morning."

In the living room, I got my piano books out of their denim bag. Even if I practiced for a half hour, I'd still have time to read.

By the time I'd finished, Dad and Luke were back in the kitchen. Dad handed us each a Rice Krispie bar wrapped in Saran Wrap. "Put these in your backpack for snack. You guys need anything else?"

"Nope." I shook my head. "What about John?"

"I gave him his last warning." Dad's voice was stern.

"But if he misses his ride, how will he get to school?"

Dad ran hot water into the sink and squirted in dish soap. "If he can't get himself up, he'll just have to miss school with an unexcused absence."

It looked like my older brother was headed for John Calvin Vos trouble.

Dad let Luke color in a Spiderman coloring book at the kitchen table, so he could keep an eye on him while he cleaned up the pancake mess. I guess he figured the dishwasher couldn't handle the stuck-on batter and syrup. He let me read in the den, but he interrupted every five minutes to tell me how much time was left before we had to walk to the bus stop. I finally gave up and quit. I went to get out our coats and boots.

John shuffled into the kitchen. A striped wool blanket draped around his shoulders and dragged on the floor behind him. He looked like Chief Geronimo, minus the headdress, although his hair stuck up almost as much as feathers. His eyes were two slits above his frown. I wished those pretty Howard twins could see him now.

He yawned. "Is there any coffee?"

"Coffee?" Dad scowled at him. "When did you start drinking coffee?"

"I thought this morning might be a good time."

"Forget it." Dad drained the dirty dishwater. "I'm not making coffee to satisfy your latest whim."

"It's not my latest whim." John clutched his tribal blanket tighter. "It's my new habit."

"It can't be your habit if you don't start. And you're not starting this morning."

"What's for breakfast then?"

I walked into the room. "It *was* blueberry pancakes, but you missed it."

Luke piped up. "I had a smiley face and a number five."

John's mouth turned down like a clown's and he rubbed an eye, pretending to cry. "I'm so-o-o-o sad I didn't get a smiley face pancake."

"I suggest helping yourself to a slice of toast." Dad's voice was as cool as the ice outside.

John pulled a face. "What about bacon and eggs?"

"You don't have time." Dad pointed to the clock. "You can either eat or shower. Your ride's going to be here in about fifteen minutes."

John frowned. "Isn't school cancelled?"

"Two-hour delay." Dad's lips made a tight line. "Do the math."

John looked at the clock. "Two-hour delay—" He jerked. "Oh, wow. I'll shower now and take a piece of toast with me." He stuck a slice of bread in the toaster and ran to the bathroom.

Dad sighed as he wiped his hands. "And I still haven't started sermon preparation." He looked at us. "Bundle up, guys. You can walk over to the bus stop now."

After we put on our coats, Dad hugged us. "Bye, Matt. Bye, Luke. Have a great day."

I pulled my backpack over my shoulders. "You too, Dad."

Dad went into his study. I opened the back door and Luke ran out. His feet shot out from under him, and he fell on his back with a thump!

32

SLIP-SLIDING

Luke was so surprised that he didn't move or cry. He looked like a dead fish, staring at the sky with wide eyes. His backpack must have cushioned his fall.

I grabbed his arm and pulled him up. "The sidewalks are icy." I grabbed his hand. "Hang on and walk slow." *I can't believe I just said that to Luke Slow Walker.*

We slid along the slick sidewalk to the corner. Every twig on each tree was coated with ice. A city truck rumbled past, dumping sand from its raised bed. The street was slushy, but the sidewalk was coated with a layer of ice that looked like a thin sheet of glass.

I pretended I walked on the glass roof of a warehouse, on a secret mission to find out if the enemy was making bombs. I slid my feet across the panes, looking for signs of weapon manufacturing on the cement floor below.

"Good morning, guys."

I jumped and turned around. It was Jenny, but I was happy to see she was minus Brutus.

"Morning, Jenny. Nice day for a skate, isn't it?"

She laughed. "It is." She ran on the grass, jumped on the sidewalk, and slid past us.

I tugged Luke's hand. "C'mon, Luke. Walk on the grass."

Luke didn't move. "We're not supposed to walk on the grass."

"Since when did not being allowed to do something ever stop you?" I jerked him off the sidewalk. "See, the grass isn't so slick. We can move faster."

Each blade of grass was covered with a thin layer of ice. It was like I was a huge giant stomping on the tiny spears of a miniature army.

By the time we caught up to Jenny, she was at the bus stop. Dan, Josh, and Mike were there, too. They must have watched Jenny slide up because they were all running on the grass and jumping onto the sidewalk.

Dan yelled at Josh. "Ha! I slid farther than you."

"No way!" Josh gestured wildly with his arms. "I slid past three cracks and you only went past two."

Jenny did a dance and leaped onto the sidewalk. She glided a long way, putting up her arms and twirling like a ballerina. She laughed. "I don't think you guys know anything about ice skating."

"Hey, look." Josh pointed at us. "The PKs are here."

"Don't answer," I said to Luke. "Just ignore him."

"Okay." Luke let go and slid to the little kids.

Josh yelled a sing-song. "PK-2. How are you?"

I walked right past him. "Hello, Mike. Hello, Dan. Nice morning, isn't it?"

Mike grinned. "Any morning with two hours less school is a nice morning."

Dan frowned. "It would be nicer if we were ice fishing instead of going to school."

Jenny slid up to us. "Now Matt knows all about skating." She grabbed my hands and pulled me onto the sidewalk with her. "C'mon, Matt, skate with me."

My feet slipped and I tried to fling out my arms to keep my balance, but Jenny had my hands locked in a viselike grip. I began falling backward and jerked her toward me. She pulled back. Her feet slipped forward and knocked mine out from under me. She fell flat on her back and I landed on top of her!

Josh whistled. Dan yelled and slapped his leg. "Matt, the lady-killer!"

Mike laughed. "That was too funny." But he gave me his hand and pulled me up.

"Thanks, Mike." I turned to help Jenny. She was curled into a ball, holding her stomach and shaking. I bent down. "Are you okay?"

She looked up through strands of dark hair. "Oh, Matt!" She burst out laughing. "I'm sorry, but you should have seen your face."

Mike grinned. "That whole dance was hilarious." He held up his hands and pretended he was cranking an old-time movie camera. "I wish I had a video of it."

Josh punched his arm. "You could send it in to 'America's Funniest Home Videos.'"

"Yeah!" Dan fist-pumped the air. "I bet you'd win the $10,000."

Jenny pushed her hair back into her hood. "Matt, you may be a good skater, but you need dancing lessons."

The school bus came around the corner and put on its flashing red lights, saving me from trying to explain why no boy on earth would want to take piano lessons and dancing lessons.

33
A LITTLE GOOD NEWS

We had a ton of homework because classes were shorter due to our late start, and hardly any teacher gave us time to work on assignments. On the bus after school, Josh and I did our math together. That went so fast, we did our history assignment together, too.

When Luke and I walked into the house, Mom was folding laundry on the kitchen table. "Hello, boys. How was school?"

I pulled books from my backpack. "Fine."

Luke dropped his mittens on the floor. "Good." He kicked off his boots. "I'm hungry. Can I have popcorn?"

Mom sighed. "You *may*." She put a bag of popcorn in the microwave, and when it dinged she poured some into bowls for Luke and me. He ate his while watching his favorite show about a little dog named Wishbone. I sat at the kitchen table and ate mine while reading the next chapter in my science textbook.

Dad came out of his study. "Any of that popcorn left?"

"A little." Mom folded washcloths into neat stacks.

This was my chance. "Did you two talk about the Camporee today?"

Dad poured some popcorn into a bowl. "We did talk about it, but we didn't have time to go over bills. We're going to work on that tomorrow."

"What should I tell my counselor?"

Mom picked up the folded towels and washcloths and headed for the bathroom. "If he asks, you'll just have to tell him your parents are still considering it."

My wide eyes begged Dad for another answer. He had a mouthful of popcorn, so he just shrugged and went to the study. I sighed and went back to my homework.

For English, I had to choose a writing assignment. I could either write about my favorite teacher (*forget that*) or an object that was important to me (*like what?*) or where I'd travel if I could go anywhere (*bingo!*).

Quickly, I wrote my title on a blank page: KAMP KANANASKIS IN ALBERTA.

I wrote about all the cool stuff boys did at the International Cadet Camporee, like working together to build a shelter. I said that I wanted to fly on a jet and see mountains. My last sentence was, "I only hope my Mom and Dad can afford the $500 so I can go."

As I signed my name in my best cursive, I sighed with satisfaction. My personal mountain of homework was finished. I headed up the stairs to find my book.

The back doorbell rang before I got to my room, so I turned to go down and answer it.

But Dad beat me to it. I heard him say, "Fred, good to see you. Come in. Let me take your jacket."

It must be Mr. Winters.

Mom came up from the basement and asked, "Would you like a cup of coffee?"

"No, thanks," Mr. Winters said. "Don't bother."

I hopped down the rest of the steps and into the kitchen. Mr. Winters sat at the table with his Army jacket hanging on the back of a chair.

I gathered up my homework from the table. "Hi, Mr. Winters."

"Hiya, Matt. How's it goin'?"

"Great. I'm already done with homework and I practiced piano this morning."

"Good work, soldier." Mr. Winters gave me a snappy salute. "What're you going to do with all your free time this evening?"

"Cadets." I raised my voice. "We'll probably hear more about Camporee. That's when thousands of Cadets from all over the United States and Canada camp for a week in the mountains."

"Sounds like a bunch of fun." Mr. Winters grinned. "Bet you're really excited."

"I don't know yet if I'm going." I glanced at my parents from the corners of my eyes.

Mom cleared her throat. "We're thinking about it."

Dad looked at the ceiling. "We'll probably make a decision tomorrow."

Mr. Winters looked from one to the other. "Oh."

John ran through the back door, singing loudly. "There's nothin' I can do—I been lookin' for a girl like you—" He snapped shut his lips and skidded to a stop. His eyes swept over us as his face flamed redder. "'Only Wanna Be With You' by Hootie and the Blow Fish."

I thought he might get into trouble, but Dad only smiled. "Hi, John." He seemed glad for the interruption. Maybe so he could steer the subject away from the Camporee. "Mr. Winters just dropped in. Why don't you microwave some popcorn for a snack?"

Luke came in from the den and held out his bowl. "I want more popcorn."

"You've had enough." Mom took his bowl. "I don't want you to spoil your appetite."

John's voice and face color had returned to normal. "What's for dinner?"

"I have a tuna casserole ready to go in the oven." Mom turned toward Mr. Winters. "Would you like to stay? We'll have plenty."

"No, no, I can't stay." Mr. Winters held up a hand. He probably felt the same way I did about tuna casserole. "I just wanted to return Pastor Tim's book." He held it out.

I crooked my neck to read the title: *Desiring God* by John Piper.

Dad took it from him. "What did you think?"

"It blew me away." Mr. Winters fingered his one gold earring. "I can't wrap my brain around the idea of pleasing God by delighting in him. I guess I always thought of God more like a grouchy old man who didn't like to see kids having any fun."

"God is our father." Dad smiled. "And most fathers like to see their children enjoying themselves—as long as they're not doing something wrong."

"It's tough for me to imagine God wanting me to enjoy life. I'd like to talk about it, but I don't want to horn in on your supper." Mr. Winters slipped on his jacket. "I'll call you later."

Mr. Winters saluted me again on his way out the door.

Mom was right about that tuna casserole. We had plenty. I don't think John and Luke cared for it much either, but even Luke knew better than to say anything.

We'd learned long ago that anyone who complained about the food got another helping.

At Cadets, I shook my head sadly when my counselor asked if I'd registered yet. Would Mom and Dad ever make up their minds?

When I got back home, I took my bedding out of the closet and sighed. How long would I have to keep doing this? If we didn't move into a bigger house, Mom might make me go back to sleeping with Luke. I'd rather make my bed every night and put away my stuff every morning than sleep with that hit and spit machine.

John came into the den, holding a cookie in each hand. He handed one to me.

"Hey, thanks." I sat on my blankets and bit the cookie. "Chocolate chip—my favorite."

John sat on the sofa arm. "You know." He munched and talked at the same time. "I've been thinking more about being a junior counselor at Camporee."

I sat up straighter. "If you go, John, it will cost Mom and Dad twice as much."

"Yeah." John nodded. "I don't think they can afford that."

"I'm not even sure they can afford to send me."

"I wonder about that too. They're definitely taking their time deciding."

"Did it take them this long when you went to Camporee three years ago?"

"No." John shook his head. "I think we sent in my registration form the next day."

"The longer they take to make up their minds, the more likely they are to say no."

"That's usually the way it works." John popped the last of his cookie into his mouth.

"Yeah."

"Tell you what." He stood, brushing cookie crumbs onto my blanket. "I just won't mention the junior counselor thing. It would be awesome to go white-water rafting, but you're right. I've had my chance to go to Camporee, even if it was only in Michigan."

"Thanks, John. I really appreciate that."

At least he's not going to spoil it for both of us. Now if only Mom and Dad will decide they can afford it. If only they will let me go!

34

SINCERE DESIRE

After breakfast the next morning, I peeked in the open door of Dad's study. He looked up and saw me. "Hi, Matt. All ready for school?"

"Just about. I wanted to ask you a question."

"Come on in."

I stood stiffly in front of his desk. How could I tell him how much going to Camporee meant to me?

Dad pushed back his chair and looked at me. "What's on your mind, kiddo?"

I took a deep breath. "It's about Camporee." All my feelings gushed out like a rushing waterfall. "I know $500 is a lot and I know we don't have much money for extra things and that we're going to have more expenses with a new baby and I know that life isn't always fair, but it already doesn't seem fair that I don't get a room of my own just because some people at church didn't vote for the proposal and now I have to keep sleeping on the den sofa and I am sick of it, but there's no way I want to go back to sleeping with motion machine Luke and I am tired of always having to do the work, but never getting to do anything fun and John got to go to Camporee and—and—"

I looked at Dad. He was smiling a tiny smile and his eyes were soft.

I swallowed and said quietly, "—and—and I just wish I could go."

Dad smiled a little more. "You finished?"

"I guess so." What else could I say?

Dad stood up. "Believe it or not." He came around his desk. "I really do understand how you feel." He scooted a chair next to me. "When I was growing up, I shared a bed with Uncle Luke, who was a terribly restless sleeper."

"Too bad you named my little brother after him."

"It does seem Luke inherited his sleeping behaviors." Dad angled the chair closer. "Anyway, I had to bunk with that active brother until I went to college."

"That's just what I'm afraid of—"

He twisted to face me. "But now that my brothers and I are adults, we're best of friends. Maybe someday you'll be buddies with your brothers, too."

"Maybe." I wasn't going to hold my breath.

Dad leaned forward. "I understand how much you want to go to Camporee. I want you to go, too." He took hold of my arms and looked in my eyes. "Mom and I will crunch some numbers this morning and see what we can figure out. Okay?"

"Okay."

"But, Matt." Dad pulled me closer. "I believe you have to start thinking differently about things. You should stop thinking so much about yourself and what you want. Try to think more about God and what he wants."

I stiffened. "Doesn't God want me to have fun? You and Mr. Winters were talking last night about how God likes to see his children enjoying life."

"God is pleased when we find our joy in him." Dad nodded. "Do you find joy in doing what God wants, Matt? Or are you happy only when you get your way?"

I should have known better than to try to talk to Dad.

"It's a tough question. One we all struggle with—no matter what our age. How about we pray together?"

That was Dad's usual answer for problems. But I nodded.

"Gracious heavenly Father." Dad took a deep breath. "You know our hearts. And you know our deepest desires. You are the God who delights in giving his children every good and perfect gift. Help us to find joy— not in the things we have or do, but in loving and serving you. We pray this in the name of your Son, Jesus Christ, who loves us so we can love others. Amen."

"Amen," I echoed.

Dad finally let go of me and leaned back. "Matt, you may think that it stinks to have a preacher for a dad because he always seems to answer your questions by praying about them—"

The way he read my mind sometimes was spooky.

"I remember feeling the same way at your age." Dad chuckled. "I told myself that if I ever had kids I wouldn't cop out of all their questions by praying about them. But here I am—doing the same thing. You know why?"

"No." I shook my head. "Why, Dad?"

"Because prayer is powerful. And God wants us to lay our cares and concerns on him. The older I get, the more I see the value of prayer and praying with my kids."

Dad rubbed my hair. "But I promise you, Matt, Mom and I will do everything we can today to try to send you to Camporee."

"Thanks, Dad."

"In the meantime, you do what you can to think differently, all right?"

"All right."

I brought *The Voyage of the Dawn Treader* with me on the bus. I opened it as soon as I sat down beside Josh. I pretended to read, but my mind raced a million miles per hour.

Do I think too much about myself? It doesn't seem like anyone else is thinking about me and the things I want. If I don't think about myself, who will?

I immediately felt guilty. I knew that Mom and Dad loved me and cared about me. They'd be happy to send me to Camporee if they could afford it.

Lord, forgive me for thinking so much about myself. Help me to think more about you and other people.

"So, Josh." I closed my book and put it away. "What did you choose for that writing assignment?"

ANSWERED PRAYER

School was finally over. Josh wasn't riding the bus, so I could read *The Voyage of the Dawn Treader* without being interrupted.

The ship's crew explored a small island where they found a lost lord—as a golden statue in the bottom of a lake! The water turned things into gold. Caspian tested it by dipping a plant into the water. When he pulled it out, every part that had gotten wet had turned into solid gold.

I looked out the bus window. *I would love to go to that island and dip some plants in that lake. I'd give the gold to Mom and Dad and they'd never have to worry about money again.*

Then I read about how Caspian and Edmund argued and how Lucy yelled and complained.

Maybe it's true what Dad says about the love of money being the root of all evil.

Seeing Aslan made the children forget their quarrels and most of what had happened. My favorite character, the brave mouse, Reepicheep, named that bad island "Deathwater."

The bus braked and I looked up. It was my stop. I shoved my book in my bag and hopped off the bus. What had Mom and Dad decided about Camporee?

I was glad it wasn't Luke's day for school so I didn't have to walk slowly. I ran all the way to our house and through the back door. "Mom! Dad! I'm home."

They sat at the table, holding cups of steaming tea and smiling at me. "Well, hello, Matt." Dad grinned. "Are you especially eager to be home for some strange reason?"

"You know why." I hurried to them, still wearing my coat. "What did you decide?"

Mom smiled. "You can go, Matt."

"I can? Whoopee!" I hooted and hollered. I danced a little victory jig. Then I stopped and looked at them. "Sure you can afford it?"

"Sit down, Matt." Dad pulled out a chair. "We want to tell you something."

I slipped off my backpack and coat. I looked from Dad's grin to Mom's Mona Lisa smile.

She wrapped her fingers around her cup. "Dad and I sat down together before lunch." She became very serious. "We went over all our expected expenses for the next few months and compared it to our income."

Dad no longer grinned. "We just didn't see how we could swing an extra $500."

"We talked about if it had been only the $200, we might be able to do it." Mom sipped her herbal tea. "But over $500? We just couldn't come up with that much."

Dad nodded. "We were pretty discouraged." He rubbed his chin. "We tried to think of corners we could cut, but it seemed we'd already cut every possible one."

Mom jumped back in. "So we decided to look at it again after we ate."

"And we prayed about it during devotions at lunch."

"In fact, we did something we'd never done before." Mom took a deep breath.

I looked from one parent to the other and put up my hands. "What?"

Mom said, "We asked God for a specific amount of money."

"You did?" I'd never heard anyone ask for money in a prayer. "How much?"

"Well." Dad ran his fingers through his hair. "We actually asked for $500."

I widened my eyes. "Really?"

Mom put down her cup. "But we told God we'd be happy even if he didn't give it to us."

"After we cleared the table, the telephone rang." Dad looked at me. "It was Mr. Loursma."

This wasn't making any sense. "The old—I mean—the older man?"

Dad shook his head. "No, the younger Mr. Loursma. Tom."

"Okay." I wanted to get to the good part. "Go on."

"Anyway." Dad cleared his throat. "Mr. Loursma is chairman of the deacons."

I was getting more confused and impatient. *What on earth does the younger Mr. Loursma have to do with me going to Camporee?* "And?"

"Mr. Loursma said—" Dad seemed to enjoy dragging this out— "that someone anonymously gave a gift of $500 for the pastor's family. He planned to deposit it this afternoon, and wondered if we preferred for him to put it into our savings or our checking account."

My jaw dropped. "You're kidding."

"No." Mom shook her head. "It's absolutely true. God provided exactly what we needed just when we needed it. Now we have the money for you to go to the Camporee."

"Mr. Loursma deposited the funds and I wrote the check." Dad waved it in the air. "Let's fill out your registration form and get this in the mail."

"All right!" I jumped up and hugged my parents. "Thanks, Mom. Thanks, Dad."

"Don't thank us." Mom rubbed my hair. "The thanks go to someone else, but we don't know who."

"In the final analysis, the thanks go to God." Dad tapped the check. "He's the one who worked in the heart of this person to give this specific amount at this particular time."

I still couldn't get over it. "Exactly $500." I sank back onto my chair. "That's amazing!"

"It is." Mom grasped my hand. "I think we ought to give credit to whom credit is due."

"I agree." Dad reached out for Mom's hand and mine. He bowed his head. "Let's pray."

Dad thanked God for this marvelous gift. He asked him to bless me and keep me safe when I went to the Camporee. He asked God to help me grow in wisdom and knowledge as I continued my journey through life. Then he squeezed my hand and said, "Amen."

I looked at Mom's eyes, glistening with tears, and Dad's face-splitting grin. The decision had been made. My wait was finally over.

But my adventure was only beginning.

THINKING THINGS THROUGH

Who was your favorite character in this story? Why?

When we first meet Matthew, he's worried about many different things. What do you worry about, and how does trusting God help you overcome your worry?

Matthew discovers more about Mrs. Miller and Mr. Houser when he visits them. Why might it help you appreciate older people if you heard their stories?

In this story, Matthew struggles to get along with several people. What causes conflict between you and your friends or family members? What can you do to make those relationships better?

How does thinking more about others and less about yourself help improve your attitude and relationships?

HIDING GOD'S WORD IN YOUR HEART

You may want to memorize some of these Bible verses.

For when you worry:
Cast all your anxiety on him because he cares for you.
1 Peter 5:7

For when you are afraid:
When I am afraid, I will trust in you.   Psalm 56:3

To remind you of God's great love:
For God so loved the world that he gave his one and only Son, that whoever believes in him shall not perish but have eternal life.   John 3:16

Trust:
Some trust in chariots and some in horses, but we trust in the name of the LORD our God.   Psalm 20:7

Trust in the LORD with all your heart and lean not on your own understanding; in all your ways acknowledge him, and he will make your paths straight.   Proverbs 3:5-6

35009892R00125

Made in the USA
Charleston, SC
26 October 2014